A master of the cliffhanger, creating scene after scene of mounting suspense and revelation . . . Heart-whamming.

— **PUBLISHERS WEEKLY**

A master of suspense.

— **LIBRARY JOURNAL**

One of the best writers out there, bar none.

— **IN THE LIBRARY REVIEW**

There'll be no sleeping till after the story is over.

— **JOHN GILSTRAP**, NYT BESTSELLING AUTHOR

James Scott Bell's series is as sharp as a switchblade.

— **MEG GARDINER**, EDGAR AWARD WINNING AUTHOR

One of the top authors in the crowded suspense genre.

— **SHELDON SIEGEL**, NYT BESTSELLING AUTHOR

ROMEO'S WAY

A Mike Romeo Thriller

JAMES SCOTT BELL

Compendium Press

ROMEO'S WAY

Sing, goddess, the wrath of Achilles ...
  – Homer, *The Iliad*

Everybody has a plan until they get punched in the face.
  – Mike Tyson

IT WAS THE first Tuesday in March, the sun taking its sweet time fighting off the cloud cover and recent rains, when I saw the kid who wanted to die.

I like to run the high ground in the mornings, even with the narrow roads and the anxious commuters popping from driveways and curbsides in a malignant hurry, trying to beat the mass of their own ilk to the freeway onramps. It's sort of a game with me. The Benz backing out into the street becomes a challenge—do I bank right or left to avoid the tail? It forces a quick think, and I'm all about the quick think.

The smell of laurel and sage is best right after a rain. Especially in L.A., where so many scents duke it out. Street smells and sky smells, perfumed maidens on Rodeo Drive and cologned lawyers in Superior Court. East Los Angeles hot dogs cooked on grills with onions and bacon, and smoke in your nose when the hills are on fire. That would happen in a couple of months, these same hills that now smelled so sweet. The vegetation would dry to a crispy brown and the firebugs would come out. It's people that set the hills on fire. That's what they never tell you.

I'd just come down to the flatlands of Los Feliz, a nice sweat working through my T-shirt, when I noticed a boy of about ten with his hand on a telephone pole. He was rocking back and forth. He wore jeans that were fraying at the cuffs. Little white strands from the jeans tickled his black high-top Converse shoes. His right foot was set behind and his knees were slightly bent. It was the look of a wide receiver at the line of scrimmage.

If he was going to run across the street, he should have been gone. But he wasn't moving. He was looking around the pole, down the street—his back was to me—as if hiding from something. Or waiting for something to come along.

Something like a car going a little too fast for this residential area. I heard it before I saw it. A red BMW powering down from the intersection. It was maybe a hundred yards away from where the kid was.

I was half a block from him. I knew then what he wanted to do. I didn't yell because it might have scared him into the street. I had to get to him in time to snag him.

Geometry and physics were never my favorite subjects. I liked hanging out with Descartes and Spinoza. I was never going to be an engineer or systems designer. But you get the principles stuffed into your head and they can come in handy in the strangest of places.

Like calculating how to get to a kid before a car does.

I sprinted.

The boy was tensing, like a lion taking a bead on a gazelle. He didn't have anything in his hands. It wasn't a prank he was about to pull. There could be only one reason he was getting ready to make a dash. I didn't have time to analyze it, to wonder what was making a ten-year-old want to leave life. That was usually the province of angst-ridden teenagers and end-of-the-line adults. He was too young for this.

The BMW, as they often do, decided it was a good time to speed up. There is a pecking order of cars in Los Angeles and the BMW considers itself the prize peacock. When it can get away with flouting the speed limit, it usually does.

Especially the red ones. What is it about red that brings out the gas-happy foot?

I was late getting to the kid.

I HAD TO veer into the street and make one last leap for the finish line.

The kid was two steps off the curb when I grabbed a handful of his T-shirt.

The car didn't even slow. I caught a quick look at the driver, a woman with tight hair, looking down at her lap.

I held the kid up, his arms and legs wiggling wildly in the air.

"Lemme go!" he shrieked.

I felt like a Maine lobsterman holding up a five pounder. I walked him back to the telephone pole and sat him on the ground.

"What are you doing that for?" I said.

He had tears in his eyes. His hair was black and his skin brown. His eyes were a deeper brown and should have had innocence in them, not the wetness of despair. And not the something else I saw—the kind of fear that no kid should have to experience. It wasn't the being-scared-of-the-dark kind of fear, because that goes away with the light. It was the fear that there was no light at all.

"Come on, man," I said. "You don't want to do that." I sat cross-legged in front of him.

He tried to get up then but I was ready for him. He was skinny and I grabbed his jeans pocket and snatched him back to the ground.

"Hey!" he said.

"Hey what?"

"You can't do that!"

"I'm not going to hurt you," I said. "I just don't think you should splatter your guts on a car."

He looked surprised, like I'd peered into his brain.

"Yeah," I said, "what were you thinking?"

"Let me go," he said, quietly this time.

"I want to know what you were thinking. Do you think?"

"Huh?"

"Think." I tapped the side of my head. "Up here."

"Come on, lemme go."

"We're going to think first. Then I might let you go."

For the first time he looked deeply at me, up and down. "Who are you?"

"I'm from around here," I said. "And I don't want my streets painted with blood. It's not a good look."

The kid looked at his shoes.

"You a basketball player?" I said.

He shrugged.

"Who do you like?"

He shrugged again.

"All right, let's do it this way," I said. "You tell me why you think it's a good idea to get smashed by a car, and I'll tell you what I think of that idea."

More tears came from the kid's eyes. He made a half-hearted attempt to get up again, but I pulled him right back down. That made him cry harder.

"All right," I said. "Let it out for ten more seconds. I'll wait."

That made him stop almost immediately. He wiped the tears away with his hands and then his nose with his forearm.

"I'll let you in on something," I said. "Most of the great men of the world thought about offing themselves at one time or another."

A look of interest crept into his eyes. That was a good sign. A little bit to hook him. Don't reel him in too soon. I could almost hear my dad's voice telling me that very thing out on Chesapeake Bay. Play the fish a little, don't be ham-fisted.

"There was a guy named Søren Kierkeaard who thought about it," I said.

"Who?"

"Crazy name, huh?"

"Yeah."

"What's your name?"

"Henry."

"I'm Mike." I put my hand out. He took it. Good.

"So this guy, Søren, he became one of the great thinkers. You know, there are people whose only job it is to go around thinking. They're called philosophers."

Henry said nothing.

"So here's the thing, why he didn't do it. He thought to himself, you know, why not try to look at what I'm doing, think about it, figure out what it means, then write that down. Why waste my despair?"

"Des what?"

"Sadness. Everybody gets sad."

"You ever want to?" Henry asked.

I nodded. "I wasn't that much older than you. I'm glad didn't."

"But you're strong," he said.

"Strong?"

"You can fight."

I homed in on that answer and put some things together. "Is that what this is about? Are you getting beat up?"

He said nothing.

"At school?" I said.

He was staring at his shoes again, picking at the bottom of one with his hand.

"You can be strong," I said.

He looked up.

"Let me tell you about strong. It's not just outside but inside. You have to have both. And you can. Anybody can."

"I'm too small," he said.

"You know what?"

"What?"

"When I was your age, I was the fat kid. I didn't have any strength in my arms."

"What happened?"

"Later on I figured it out. I worked the body and the mind. You ever heard of the Greeks?"

He shook his head.

"They had the idea you should work out your mind and work out your body. And learn to wrestle."

"Wrestle?"

"Not like the stuff you see on TV. That's bogus."

"It is?"

"Totally. It's an act. I'm talking about real wrestling, taking someone down. You can learn to do that. You ever heard of MMA?"

He nodded.

"You can learn that stuff," I said.

"Where?"

"Around."

"You know it?"

"Some."

"Could you show me?"

The spark of an old idea flicked in my brain. I'd thought about it before, starting a studio for kids, combining body and mind. It would be MMA and chess. Codes of conduct as well as methods of takedown. A dream, but not one I really thought would happen. There was too much baggage around me, and I was not the kind meant for settling in one place. Even though I was here with Ira, and he was the only one I could truly call friend, I didn't know if I was going to be staying in Los Angeles.

"I could show you a couple of moves," I said. "But you'd have to practice. And you'd have to learn how to use what I show you. You can't abuse it. You'd have to promise me that. You promise?"

He nodded.

"Let me hear you say it."

"I promise."

I shook his hand again. "A handshake seals a deal."

"Okay."

"Now stand up and let's have a look—"

"Henry!" A woman was charging down the sidewalk toward us. She was a thirtyish Latina with long, black hair and a face set in angry stone.

"Uh-oh," Henry said.

She was on top of us like a lioness. "Why aren't you in school?"

Henry looked at the ground.

"Who are you?" the woman said to me.

"Name's Mike, I live—"

"What are you doing talking to my son, putting your hands on him?"

"It's okay, Mom—"

"Answer me, or I'll call the police."

"I'm a neighbor," I said. "I just met Henry and—"

"Come on," she said, grabbing Henry's hand. He yanked out of her grip. She made another move for him but he took off running.

"Henry!"

"Could I have a word?" I said.

"Don't you talk to him," she said.

"You're upset."

She turned and started walking away.

"He's being bullied," I said.

That turned her around. "You don't know anything! What gives you the right to talk to my son?"

"It's called neighborliness," I said. "People used to be like that."

"I don't want to see you anywhere near—"

"He needs to learn to defend himself."

"Don't you tell me what he needs! If I see you around him again, I will get the police. I will get a restraining order."

"You don't have to get anything," I said. "I'm done here."

And I was.

It was time. Time to go. Head out. Hit the road. Find a place where there were no people. The desert. Yes, find a place in the desert and become a hermit and grow a beard and occasionally scare campers. That's what I'd be good at. Live with the jackrabbits and rattlesnakes. Maybe call up some Native American spirit and learn to dance for rain. Become a shaman, dress in skins.

Nothing for you here, Romeo.

Time to leave.

"NOTHING," I SAID to Ira when I slammed the door and he

asked me what was wrong. I walked past the front room, where two other men were sitting with him.

"Mike," Ira said, "come and meet—"

"Not now," I said and went to my room. I closed the door and went in to take a shower before Ira could knock and ask me to come out.

The water was warm and good but offered no relief. I kept seeing that kid Henry. I kept imagining the bullies in his life, and seeing the ones who'd been in mine, almost drowning me once in a toilet bowl and ripping my underwear with a nuclear wedgie. I couldn't do anything about it then. I can now.

Henry needed to know how.

My left little finger started to throb in the hot water. It was still getting used to being reattached after a guy cut it off with a knife. I had to talk a doctor into sewing it back on. He said the odds were against it working again.

But my little finger is as stubborn as I am and was making a play to rejoin the other nine as a full member of the choir. I flexed it a few times. It didn't go all the way yet. It wasn't making a true fist. But close enough for me.

When I was dry and dressed I pulled out my duffel bag and started packing. I didn't know where I was going, just knew it wasn't going to be anywhere with a lot of people. I thought about heading to Union Station and taking a train somewhere. Trains are classic. Who knows how much longer they're going to be around? But you get on one and ride where the rails lead. I could pretend I was Cary Grant in *North by Northwest*.

My bag was almost fully loaded when Ira pushed open my door. He was sitting in his wheelchair like the Cheshire Cat. I hate that look. It means he knows what I'm thinking.

"Rude," he said.

"Abrupt," I said.

"I want you to meet a couple of gentlemen."

"Thanks, no."

"Now that's not very neighborly of you."

I snapped him a look. Why did he choose that word? Maybe he really could read my thoughts. Was it because he'd once been Mossad, a man who looked in eyes before he killed, and then a man who studied Torah so deep he became a rabbi and made his penance with the things of God? He'd seen more things than any ten men put together, and maybe that was why he could see into me. Another good reason to get out of town.

"I'll say hello," I said, "just to be neighborly, but then I'm heading out."

"Maybe you won't. Come on."

HE WHEELED HIMSELF back. I followed his yarmulked head to the living room. It was, like all the other rooms in Ira's house, filled with bookshelves. He'd lost count of his collection of books at seven thousand, with a few thousand of those in storage.

The two men got up from chairs. One was white and one was black. Same height and build, but there the similarities ended.

The white guy had sandy hair beating a major retreat from his forehead, an oval face, and close-set eyes. His smile was a little goofy, but those eyes made it appear more sinister. He was a man who knew where the bodies were buried. He wore a dark-red tie and a navy-blue sport coat, khaki slacks, and brown slip-on shoes. He was maybe fifty years old.

The black gentleman had a square face and thick glasses in black frames. He was older than the other guy, maybe by ten years. He wore a gray suit that was in the last stage of rumple and a tie slightly askew. I knew this look from long years of seeing it in my parents' house. He was total academia.

But his smile was warm and sincere.

"I'm Teodor Steadman," the white guy said, extending his hand to me. We shook. "And this is Samuel Johnson."

I shook Johnson's hand. "Is he your Boswell?" I said.

"Very good," Johnson said. "Not many people know that Samuel Johnson anymore."

"Is that how you got the name?"

"No, my mother just liked the sound of Samuel."

"So you're the Quixote tilting at the windmills of California," I said.

"That's the nicest thing I've been called in quite some time," Johnson said.

"Sit, sit," Ira said. He had a coffee service on a table, leaned over and poured me a cup.

"I'm not staying," I said.

"For one cup," Ira said. "You can spare me that. We'd like your input on something."

"We?"

"Ira speaks very highly of you," Steadman said.

"I've got him fooled," I said.

Steadman laughed and it seemed forced. But Johnson's smile made him feel like an old friend. I could see why he did so well with people. And what had fueled his incredible rise.

What I knew about his current standing was what I'd seen in passing on news sites. An economics professor at UCLA, the one true conservative in the department, according to some. He'd taken up writing about politics and culture about ten years ago, and his book, *The Things That Matter Most*, had become a big bestseller last year. Which was about the time his name was getting tossed around as a possible challenger to California Senator Genevieve Griffin. Griffin, who had been mayor of Oakland at one time, had never lost an election.

"Do you know much about our candidacy?" Steadman asked.

"Good luck to you," I said.

That got a frown from Steadman but a good laugh from Johnson, who said, "Luck and the hand of God are what we'll need."

"What we need is a good hammer," Steadman said. "Like Thor. And we need to find the head to bang it on."

"Sounds very Nordic," I said. "Viking politics."

"Very much so," Steadman said. "This is the reality. The other side wants to chop Sam up, and they'll do it with lies."

"Politics and lying?" I said. "The very idea."

"It's so easy to do," Steadman said. "You can pipe it all over the world instantly."

"All right," I said, "what's the big lie they're telling about Mr. Johnson?"

"They've planted a story about him having an affair."

"Politics and womanizing? The very idea."

Samuel Johnson did not laugh. "I have a wife, two children, and two precious grandchildren," he said. "I'm most concerned about them."

"They with you on this running for office thing?" I said.

"All in," he said. "They knew it would be rough. They told me to go for it."

"Then all this goes with the territory," I said.

Steadman said, "We have to cut this off right here and now. We have to show they're behind it."

"Who's behind it?"

"Oh, there's a fake blog about Sam, but we all know Parsons is running it."

"Parsons?"

"Griffin's campaign manager," Steadman said. "A sleazier customer you'll never find."

"Politics and sleaze? The very—"

"That's enough, Mike," Ira said. "Don't mind him. He goes a little funny in the head sometimes."

"This isn't a laughing matter," Steadman said. "This is about the very existence of America."

My eyebrows must have gone up about four feet, with my eyes rolling behind them.

"Oh, you don't think so?" Steadman said.

"You don't want to know what I think," I said.

"I do," Johnson said.

"Uh-oh," Ira said.

"Man is doomed," I said. "That's the short answer."

"Do you really believe that?" Johnson said.

"It's the great lesson of history. We've been heading toward the end for a long time. We'll all blow up eventually. The only question is whether there'll be anything or anybody left."

"Do you believe there will be?" Johnson asked.

"I'm on the fence," I said.

"I believe," he said. "I believe in fighting for what's good and right. If we don't fight, we're no better than the other side."

"Let's put it this way," I said. "America was an experiment in world history. It went pretty well there for awhile. But it takes an informed and engaged citizenry to make it work. Look at what we have now."

"It's too great an idea to give up on," Johnson said, and I could tell he meant it with every nerve ending in his body. It would have been cruel to call him a chump.

"Why are you running," I asked, "if you had to sum it up?"

"To try to get people to see the truth."

"People have to *want* to see," I said.

"I know what you're saying. People would rather believe in sweet lies, and then turn those sweet lies into a religion. They even have their own seminaries. They're called universities."

"Stupidity is the new profundity," I said.

"I like the way you talk."

"But I'm not running for anything."

"Maybe you should."

"People are naïve," I said, "because they can get away with it. We used to call those people fools and wouldn't listen to them. Now we give them their own talk shows."

"Shouldn't we light a candle rather than curse the darkness?" Samuel Johnson said.

"The darkness has taken over the candle factories," I said. "But I wish you good luck. I'll be rooting for you."

"We'd like you to do more than that," Steadman said. "We'd like you to work for us."

"No way," I said.

"I mean for pay, actual pay."

"And I mean no, actual no."

They all looked at each other like they didn't know what to say next.

"I'm not your man," I said. "Everybody's got to believe something, but right now, all I believe is that I should get out of town."

"I don't think that's true," Johnson said. He was looking at me the way a priest might look at a wayward boy. Like Spencer Tracy staring down Mickey Rooney in *Boys Town,* with all the idealism of somebody who thinks there's good in everybody, if only you could dig it out. Maybe he really was a chump.

"Mr. Johnson" I said, "I do wish you well. But politics is not my thing. Even if Honest Abe himself came back and said he wanted to take another shot—I guess that's a bad choice of words—another *turn* on the scene, and wanted my help, I would tell him to find somebody else."

Steadman let out an audible and disappointed sigh. Obviously meant for me. "Well, Ira, I guess you were wrong."

"I guess I was," Ira said.

"Been talking behind my back?" I said.

Ira shrugged.

I stood. "A pox on every house in this whole country. All

due respect, Mr. Johnson, but maybe you should get out before they steal your soul."

"Wait a second," Johnson said. "May I ask about the tattoo on your arm?"

My left forearm, on the underside. *"Vincit Omnia Veritas,"* I said.

"Latin," Johnson said. "Something about truth and overcoming."

"That's right."

"Do you believe that, Mr. Romeo?"

"My father did."

"He sounds like a wise man."

"He was," I said. "But he's dead."

I WALKED OUT of Ira's feeling like a jerk, like a petulant boy, and not caring that I did. Then feeling rotten that I didn't care. Samuel Johnson was a sincere man, by all I could tell a good man. I wasn't crazy about Teodor Steadman. He had slick handler written all over him. I wondered how long poor Johnson was going to last in the meat grinder of California politics.

Then I realized I was walking without my duffel. Which meant I would have to go back to Ira's one more time. I wonder what Freud might have thought of that.

I wasn't ready to go back.

Then I found myself outside the Argo and wanting to see one more person before I left for good.

The Argo is a used bookstore, one of the last standing in Los Angeles. The age of the digital title was laying waste to the world of print, and the number of used books was finite. I hoped the Argo would stick around, because it had a truly good collection and one salesperson I wished I could have known better.

A skinny guy behind the counter in a faded Alice in Chains Reunion Tour T-shirt greeted me with the half smile of the barely committed.

"Is Sophie here?" I said.

His forehead furrowed. "I don't think she's coming in today."

A thudding disappointment hit me, harder than I thought it would.

"Can I give her a message?" the guy said.

"No, thanks. She brought some books to me a while ago. I wanted to thank her again."

"She should be in tomorrow."

"I'll be gone."

"Taking a trip?"

"Moving. Out of L.A."

"Bummer." He caught himself. "Or maybe not."

"I will miss your bookstore. Great selection. Maybe I'll give it one last browse."

"Do it, man."

A bookstore is the best place to be lost. There's always a volume to grab, and inside there may be pleasures awaiting, wisdom to be gained, or at least something to make you mad. If you're mad, you know you're alive, which is a good thing to know from time to time.

I browsed for half an hour, taking down random volumes— everything from Montaigne to Hunter S. Thompson. Talk about bending your mind. A rustic French essayist and a gonzo journalist whose body was a drug lab.

Somewhere in the middle was an accurate view of humanity.

To this mix I added a volume of Dr. Seuss from the children's shelf. I parked in one of the soft chairs in the store, cracked open the Seuss, and started looking to find timeless wisdom. If not that, a laugh.

Found both, in the tale of the young Zoad.

It seems this Zoad came to a fork in the road and had to figure out which one to take. He kept giving himself arguments for one, then the other. Couldn't make up his mind. Kept stopping and starting, for thirty-six and a half hours.

Finally, he comes up with the solution. He won't be a fool and take one or the other. He won't be a dunce ... instead, he'd start out for both places at once.

And that was how the Zoad who would not take a chance got nowhere at all, with a rip in his pants.

That was why I had to go, get out, move on. If I stayed in L.A. I'd get a rip in my pants. Didn't matter the direction I went, as long as I—

"A little light reading I see."

She was there. Sophie. All six feet of her, athletic trim, black-rimmed glasses over bronze, gold-flecked eyes. And her long hair the color of red maple leaves on a New England fall morning—one of my vivid childhood memories.

My blood pumped like I was about to go into a cage match. So I had a little humanity left after all. That and a couple of bucks could get me a cup of coffee for sure, but not much else.

Churchill called his depression the Black Dog, and that rabid canine has been snapping at my heels for fifteen years. He was born the day my parents were murdered. I was seventeen and didn't have any friends but them. Both were academic superstars, and I had been accepted into Yale at the age of fourteen, which put my psyche in a vise right there.

Three years went by, but I was making it through, mostly lonely, finding solace in my books. I wrestled with Aquinas, got punched in the face by Nietzsche, recovered with Pascal, was thrown again by Hume.

I enjoyed ancient history. The Greek city-states, especially Sparta and Athens. Rome and the emperors. The Mongols of the Middle Ages.

At seventeen I looked up from my books and saw actual life starting to spread out before me. I had no idea what direction to take. My parents gave their best counsel, but you know how that goes. At seventeen you don't want to hear it. There weren't any big arguments. I didn't steal a motorcycle or start smoking weed. We all thought it was a good idea for me to live in a rented room off campus. We saw each other a lot, especially when I needed clothes washed.

Still, there was that slight but discernable tension in the air when a kid is about to become an adult and the old ways of talking don't work. I saw disappointment in my father's face, and in my mother's voice, I sometimes heard a tinny note of sadness. It ripped me up, those two things. But I held it all inside.

I wish now, and all the time I wish it, that I'd told them I understood.

One day a student entered the building where my father's office was. My mother was with him at the time. The student carried two automatic weapons and a belt of ammunition. He cut down staff and students.

He killed my parents.

He turned the gun on himself when the cops got there.

I never talked about this except to Ira. But I haven't told him everything. About what happened after, why I tracked down another man and killed him for all this. I don't know if I can open up that door, even to Ira. I only know that back in New Haven, the cops want to talk to me. But I was Michael Chamberlain then.

I'm living in that netherworld of existence, nowhere to settle, nowhere to rest. I keep holding out hope maybe I can get that black dog put down, but its teeth and saliva keep showing up in my dreams and sometimes on the street. So when there's an offer of grace, like Sophie right now, I think maybe there's a chance. But reality always comes back with a

snarl. It makes choices a little dicey. It makes running seem like
the only option. And when I get a chance like this, this woman
standing here, I'm always like that Zoad.

"Stocking up," I said, getting to my feet.

"For what?"

"I'm heading out."

"Oh."

Was that a small sound of disappointment? And what if it
was? What was I going to do about it? Stick around like a
schoolboy hoping to take her to a dance?

"I'm glad I got to hang out in your store awhile," I said.

"Well, I ... if you ever come back to town, you know where
to find us."

Find. That's what you say to somebody who's lost. Find
your way out. We'll leave the light on for you. Sophie flicked
on a light, and there it was on the distant porch in the dark of
night and all I had to do was walk toward it.

She hesitated a moment, as if expecting me to speak.
When I didn't she smiled and turned and walked away, and I
watched her walk, then I slapped my right cheek and took the
copy of Montaigne to the front desk. Sophie was helping
another customer so I bought the book for four-fifty from the
Alice in Chains guy.

And decided to give Ira one more chance.

"YOUR OFFER STILL stand?" I said.

"What offer?" Ira said, turning from his monitor.

"To wait on me hand and foot," I said.

"I'm trying to recall." Ira tapped his head. "Nope, not
there."

"Then how about your place in Paradise Cove?"

"Ah," he said. "You want to live by the ocean, the life of a
beachcomber."

"No combs. Just some quiet."

"Does that mean you want to stay after all?"

"You've got one more chance to convince me," I said.

"It's a moral argument," Ira said. "Would you like some tea? I always prefer making moral arguments over tea."

"You will not coax me with civility," I said. "State your case and make it snappy."

"I will make it whip-cracking. But if it is to be a truly moral argument, we need to agree on a standard. You, my friend, do not seem to have one. I don't know where your compass is located."

"Maybe I'm just afloat," I said. "The tide carries me wherever it will."

"I don't think you believe that," he said. "And I think you're acting like a wimp."

"Is this a motivational speech now?"

"I call them like I see them. You can decide what to do with it. You want to leave now?"

Yes. And fast.

"Finish your thought," I said. "It may be the last time you see me."

"I respect Sam Johnson. He's letting himself in for a tsunami of lies and abuse from the mob. I don't like mobs, do you?"

"No one in their right mind likes a mob, unless they're part of a mob, in which case they are by definition not in their right mind."

"Well stated."

"But Samuel Johnson doesn't have to run for office," I said.

"And you don't have to walk freely on the street." Ira said. "Are you really that obtuse?"

"Did you just use the word *obtuse* on me?"

"Would you rather I called you a blockhead?" Ira said.

"No, obtuse is fine," I said. "So why am I obtuse?"

"You're trying to live alone in this world and you can't do it. You won't be able to do it, because your conscience will grind you up."

"You assume I have a conscience."

"I know you do," Ira said. "As fast as you run, you'll never get away from it."

I shrugged.

"Your sense of justice is too finely tuned," Ira said. "And you feel in your gut what Edmund Burke once said about evil."

"Burke said a lot of things."

Ira said, "When bad men combine, the good must associate, else they will fall, one by one, an unpitied sacrifice."

With the most serious look I'd ever seen on his face, he said in almost a whisper, "You can be a sacrifice if you choose, Michael. But can you sit by and watch it happen to others?"

When he said that, I thought about Henry.

"Who would I be working for?" I said.

Ira's eyebrows went up in silent but sympathetic victory. "I'm a legal advisor to the campaign. You are my investigator. So officially, it's me. But we take day-to-day orders from Steadman."

"I don't like him."

"He's very good at what he does."

"So was Machiavelli," I said.

"Samuel Johnson trusts him," Ira said.

"All right! Anything else you want to hypnotize me with, Svengali?"

"Jewish law puts a high value on honesty," Ira said. "But there are exceptions. You will recall that Caleb and Joshua entered the land as spies and were protected by the prevarication of Rahab, who is honored among our people."

"Fascinating."

"And in the Talmud, there is the protection of honest property by making a vow, a vow mind you, to thieves and dishonest tax collectors, that the property is *terumah*, of little value but to priests. Or that the property belongs to the king. And why is this permitted? You know, for you say it yourself."

"You don't owe the truth to people who lie."

"There is a robbery being committed by people who lie."

"What's being robbed?"

"A man's good name. To lie about a man's name is considered in our law to be worse than stealing property, for property can be regained, but a good name cannot."

"And all this means what?"

"You are going to do some deceiving up in San Francisco," Ira said.

"Seems like a good city for it," I said.

"Welcome back to the world."

"Temporarily," I said.

"We'll see," Ira said.

ON WEDNESDAY I met with Teodor Steadman at his office on Wilshire Boulevard. The political consulting business must have been good to him. His office was on the third floor, in the corner, and you could look out at Wilshire and the tony Hancock Park neighborhood of Los Angeles. His office was sleek and nicely furnished, with some 8 x 10s on the wall of Steadman's unmistakable smile standing next to some other toothy fellows. I recognized John McCain in one and George W. Bush in the other. His desk was a clear glass top. Everything on the desk was neat, orderly. The thing that stood out was a skull the size of a grapefruit, grinning at me.

I sat and stared at it.

"That's Osgood," Steadman said. "He reminds me every day that all this is about death."

"That's cheery," I said.

"I'm obsessed with death."

"Even cheerier."

"Death is what will happen to this country if we don't win," Steadman said.

I said, "I always thought death was that undiscovered country from whose bourn no traveler returns."

Steadman regarded me in silence, then: "Ira told me you can come up with off-the-wall comments."

"Shakespeare is off the wall?"

"Like that. How did we get on Shakespeare?"

"It's not important," I said.

"You don't seem like you really want to be here," Steadman said. "That troubles me."

"I'm troubled by other things, Mr. Steadman. Epistemology troubles me. Bad acting troubles me. Politics I don't get exercised about. But if I get a job, I will do the job."

"You're kind of a tough guy, yeah?"

"Tough is contextual," I said.

"See? There it is again. You don't talk like a regular person."

"I'm using language to communicate. Context is everything, in language and in being tough. Now what—"

"You used to fight in cage matches?" he said.

"A while ago."

"Looks like you keep in shape."

"Man's got to watch his figure."

Steadman flashed me that smile of his. It was a salesman's tooth display, designed to set at ease and retake control of a conversation. "In spite of myself, I like you. I like that you don't take bull from people."

"Is that what you're tossing?"

"Not at all, no. What about your personal life?"

"Why are you asking?"

"In my job, information is everything. I can't turn it off." He smiled again.

I said, "My personal life is not relevant to the job."

"Well, I mean, you're not married, for instance. Ever been?"

"Steadman—"

"You're much better off, is all I'm saying." He shook his head. "You know what they say, there's only one thing keeping families connected these days. Alimony."

He waited for me to laugh. I didn't.

"I used to be married to Hitler's daughter," he said.

He chuckled, trying to prompt me to laugh. I didn't.

"You have more freedom to do some things, is my point," he said.

"Man is born free, but is everywhere in chains," I said.

"What does that mean?"

"Rousseau. Real freedom is a rare commodity."

Steadman stood up behind his desk, and spun his chair around. "That's exactly right! That's what Sam's message is all about! We're in a fight for freedom, for actual liberty. Against the growing state."

"But you need people to understand what liberty is, and who can deliberate about it wisely. You don't have that anymore. You have factions, which is what Madison warned about."

"Madison?"

"*The Federalist.*"

"I haven't read that since college."

"It holds up," I said. "But going to college is no guarantee of wisdom. And without that grounding in the political philosophy of the nation, how can anybody be expected to participate wisely? Everybody ends up treading water in the mid-Atlantic."

When I was a kid my parents took me on a trip to England. I was eight. I looked out the window once. I always wanted the window seat. I wanted to see. And there was a time when the sun was going down, and I looked out and all I could see was ocean. Yes, and was afraid, wondering what would happen if the plane went down. No one would find us. Sharks would eat us. We'd sink.

Steadman said, "You think this is all for nothing, what we're doing?"

"You've got a helluva hole to dig out of. The system worked pretty well when there was a broad consensus. But politics is like cage fighting now."

"Maybe that's why you're just the man for the job. We're not giving up. So do you want to help us out or not?"

Once I start something, I finish it. That's what I told myself, and it's true, even though I knew there was a reason to stay named Sophie hanging around inside my head, and a kid named Henry, too. And yes, a little admiration for a decent man named Samuel Johnson who was making a jump into politics, only to be lied about by people who were of Steadman's professional class.

Could I work for such a man as this? Be part of a system that is so messed up it elects nimrods to various offices who then look out for the interests of their lobbyists or backers like puppets on a string?

Could a Sam Johnson beat that racket? It'd be interesting to see him try.

"Okay," I said.

"Great!" Steadman practically jumped. "Let me tell you what we're looking for." He snagged his iPod which was sitting on his desk and turned it toward me. It held a photo of a good-looking woman in a suit, arms folded and smiling confidently at the camera. There was no end to smiles around this place.

"Her name is Katarina Hogg. H-O-G-G, but pronounced like *rogue*. We refer to the men she dates as Going Hogg."

"Sweet of you."

"And if they score, they've gone Whole Hogg."

"You really talk like that?"

"It's how we keep sane," he said.

"That might not be the right term for it."

"I'll ignore that," he said. "Anyway, she's up in San Francisco. I know her, she knows me, and she knows everybody who works for me. I want you to see if you can do some volunteer work for the Griffin campaign. Kat ... Katarina would be the one to go through, but you have to be clever about it."

"Clever?"

"We all have a heightened sense of smell, Mike. For spies."

"Sounds like a John le Carré novel."

"It's like that very much indeed." He paused then, put his fingertips together and tapped them. "What I want you to do is find out everything you can about the workings up there, but especially who is behind this mystery-woman campaign against Sam."

"You want me to find out who this woman is?"

"There is no woman. It's not true."

"How do you know?"

"Because I know Sam Johnson. There's not a better, finer man in this state, this country! He's dedicated to his family, his kids, his work, and his writing. He's deeply religious."

I said, "People like that have been known to stray."

Steadman shook his head. "I have looked into his eyes on too many occasions. He's telling the truth."

I let that go. "So you want me to find out the source of the story."

"More than that," Steadman said. "I want you inside the campaign."

"How do you propose I do that?"

"Security. They are looking for security for an event up in Frisco. I want you to get in on that."

"Just walk right in?"

"You're perfect. You've got no past. Ira's told me about you. We'll create some references, and I'll tell you exactly how to get in."

"You know how?" I said, letting the skepticism sound in my voice.

"I know Kat Hogg, Mike. I know how she thinks and operates. I'm like that German soldier in *Patton* who knew how Patton thought because he studied him so thoroughly."

"So this is like war?"

Steadman nodded happily. "Exactly like war."

"What's the pay?"

"We'll cover your expenses, of course. I'll make the arrangements. And two hundred dollars a day. It will be off the books. In cash. You all right with that?"

"I'll take some now."

"You really do cut to the chase, don't you?" Steadman said.

"A couple of Cs would be nice," I said.

Steadman nodded. "Mike, when you get back, let's go have a drink. Just the two of us. You know, I used to be pretty tough, too. I still jog every morning, lift weights."

His eyes explored my face.

"I drink alone," I said.

"Think about it," Steadman said. "We could have some good talks. I have a feeling."

He turned his chair around and pulled out a metal box from the credenza. He put the box on this desk and opened it. He counted out ten twenty-dollar bills and handed them to me.

"Now meet my son," Steadman said.

"Why?"

"He's the tech side of things. He'll prep you for your trip. I'm really excited to be working with you, Mike."

I was getting less excited by the minute.

RICKY STEADMAN WAS twenty-seven and six feet of cream-colored smoothness. He had black hair and two-days' growth of beard trying hard to come through the skin rugged, but looking more like the terrycloth. He wore his blue dress-shirt untucked over light-blue designer skinny biker jeans and a pair of clean red Chucks. Hipster casual that probably took hours to match.

We were in his cubby of an office after his father had done the intros and left us.

We were not alone.

Ricky's girlfriend, Philly, had mahogany skin and hair that was a stylish dance of black curls. Her firm, curvaceous body was packed into tight jeans and an orange tank top.

"This is a burn phone," Ricky said, sliding it to me across his desk. "Use it for all communications. If it gets taken from you, there'll be no record of calls."

"Does it shoot out an oil slick?" I said.

"Huh?"

"You're like Q in the James Bond movies," I said.

"Who's Q?" Philly said.

"You know," I said. "The guy in the beginning who gives Bond all the gadgets."

She frowned.

"It's in the *old* Bond movies," Ricky said like a disapproving parent. To me he said, "Her film knowledge isn't too great."

I said, "Not everybody is going to know about Eisenstein and the Odessa Steps sequence."

Ricky frowned, empty behind the eyes.

"It's a film-knowledge thing," I said.

Philly giggled. Ricky shot her a look, then tried the same on me. "My dad said you're a little out there," he said. "I don't think you're the right guy for this job, you want to know the truth."

"You want to fire me?" I said.

"I don't have that authority," Ricky said, but clearly wished he had.

Philly said, "You used to be a cage fighter, didn't you?"

"Used to be," I said.

Ricky said, "Philly—"

"You could still do it, looks like," Philly said, and she gave me an unmistakable, primordial gleam of flirtation.

"Hey!" Ricky said. "Can we please?" He gestured, palms up. "This is a professional meeting."

"I don't mind getting to know the people I'm working for," I said.

"You don't work for her," Ricky said. "You work for me."

"You mean your dad," I said.

"For the campaign," Ricky said. "And I don't think you're going to work out."

"Why don't you call your pop and talk it over?" I said.

Philly giggled again.

"Will you please be quiet?" Ricky said.

"Don't tell me to be quiet," Philly said.

"I'm telling you now," Ricky said.

I said, "Listen, kids, I don't want to be third wheel or anything."

Philly stood up. "Forget it. I'm going. It was nice meeting you, Mike. Maybe sometime we can have a real conversation."

"I'd like that," I said.

"If you're going to go, go," Ricky said.

"Oh I'm going," she said with a defiant lilt. "Maybe I'll go all the way to Aruba. Alone." She picked up her backpack and slung it on one shoulder. She put an emphasis on her vibe with a healthy slam of the door.

"Man, she drives me crazy sometimes," Ricky said.

"Maybe you should be nicer to her," I said.

"You know, just stop now. I'm not here to get personal advice from you. I'm prepping you and that's it."

"A good relationship is worth nurturing." I said, just to razz him.

"What did I just say? You have the burner phone. Here's an iPad. I hope you know how to use an iPad."

"Shucks, I just got into the city from the farm," I said. "What do I know about your fancy gadgets?"

He flopped a file folder in front of me. I opened to a stack of papers and a white business envelope.

"Those are printed reports," he said. "Look them over before you get to San Francisco. In that envelope is two hundred cash and an ATM card. The PIN's on the back of the envelope. If you need more than a couple hundred, check in first. You have a driver's license?"

"Of course," I said. Only mine was a very nice fake, provided me by a great little procurer named Lyle Thebes.

Ricky shook his head.

"What?" I said.

"I don't like this at all," he said. "I don't know you at all, you've got no history."

"That's a good thing for a job like this."

"Whatever," Ricky said. "There's only one reason I'm going along."

"And that would be?"

"Samuel Johnson absolutely trusts Ira Rosen. And they both like you for some odd reason."

"It's my natural charm," I said.

"Right," he said with just a twinge of sadness. Maybe thinking of Philly's playful chat with me. I could understand that. No guy wants some other guy outdoing him in front of his girlfriend.

"Look," I said, "I'm being hired for a job. When I take on a job, I do it. I'm not going to implode in your face. I know how to keep my mouth shut, and if things go south, I know how to disappear. In short, we're on the same team for the time being, personal feelings aside."

Ricky was listening.

I stuck out my hand.

He paused, then took it. Weak grip.

I stood and gathered up the phone, iPad, and file. "Now go run after that girl of yours and apologize, and take her to a nice dinner."

THAT SOUNDED GOOD to me—a nice dinner. With someone new, so the anticipation of getting to know the person is a pleasure in itself. I had good dinners with Ira, but he knew me as well as anyone, which means he knows about sixty percent of me. That's my limit.

I'd like to widen that border someday.

I don't know if I can.

So a picture formed in my mind of a nice table in a corner of the kind of restaurant where they change your silverware, where the sommelier wears a little cup around his neck, and across from me is Sophie from the bookstore, and we're talking about Harper Lee or J. D. Salinger or Thomas Pynchon or Raymond Chandler.

Nice thought.

Instead, I ended up at Arby's and had their pulled-pork sandwich at a table in the middle of the place.

No one talked to me about anything.

ON THURSDAY MORNING I got on the train at Union Station in downtown L.A.

Trains are the best way for me to travel. Airports are too intrusive. Even though my identity was bought and paid for when the market for such things was more open—before 9/11 —I don't take too many chances. Besides, I like trains. The leisurely pace gives me time to think.

That's one thing people don't have much anymore, time to

think. When they are alone with their thoughts, it's nerve-racking. They're not *doing* something, so they have to fill the gap. Not with cogitating, but with doing—with tweeting and gaming and talking and checking. We're going to have an epidemic of neck problems now from all the people looking down at their phones for hours at a time.

Even on the trains now people have portable DVD players, iPods, tablets, wireless internet access. The world is not full of wonder outside the windows. It's artificially crammed into tiny visuals and earbuds.

I took my seat in business class—another Steadman expense—and settled in. I put my head back and closed my eyes until we rolled out and started chugging north. Through the San Fernando Valley then the rocks of Chatsworth and into Simi Valley, a tucked-away community still hanging on to some rural dream, even though they've overbuilt the houses.

When we hit Oxnard and started up the coast toward Santa Barbara, I figured I needed to justify my employment for a while.

I broke out the file Ricky had given me.

First item was a recent column by Samuel Johnson which appeared in *TownHall.com* and on numerous other websites. It was the one he wrote before the first rumors of extramarital dalliance were scattered. It ended with this:

We are living in the age of 'crats telling us how we must think and how we must feel. When crackpots did that on street corners, it was innocuous. But when the 'crats get into it, it's the death of the mind, the individual and that quaint little idea our founders called freedom.

And like frogs in slowly boiling water, the low information citizen will wake up one day in a prison of the mind and start to whine about it.

But by then it will be too late.

Sheep who accept being lied to should not bleat when they discover they are being fleeced.

Pretty good line, that last one. Ended the column with wry smile. But his next column, dated one week later, had a different tone:

Years ago I gave a speech at Marquette University. It was a speech about courage, about accountability and discipline, and about refusing to give up. When I was finished, a young black man stood up for a question and asked, "What real hope is there for me to advance? Why should I believe any of this?"

I almost fell over the lectern. Here we were, decades after the accomplishments of the Civil Rights movement, and I was getting a question like that.

I looked at the student and said, "When I was your age, there was a lot more discrimination than there is today. I don't recall talking about having no hope with my classmates. We talked about hard work."

But the indoctrination of young blacks continues apace, and our only hope for true justice (not the fake justice so many mouths prattle about) is to put a stop to it.

Incendiary stuff to be sure. Almost out of character for the mild-mannered man I'd met in Ira's living room. If a white guy had uttered these words, he'd be called a racist. But coming from Johnson, it was a different matter. His opponents had to choose different names.

Which is why Steadman had appended some pages he'd labeled "A sampling of the opposition."

The first page was a transcript from a show on a cable network hosted by Dr. Rodney Shipp. Shipp was well known as a civil rights "lifer" who had his own organization called Community Action Under Sacred Effort, or CAUSE. He was often compared to people like Jesse Jackson or Al Sharpton, but he apparently bristled at the comparison. He liked to call himself "the Muhammad Ali of civil rights." There was a famous picture of him with boxing gloves on punching a portrait of George W. Bush.

The transcript came from an interview Shipp conducted with Dr. Harnell Dickerson of Cornell University:

Shipp: What do you make about what Samuel Johnson said about racism in America, about it not being anything like it once was?

Dickerson: I think he needs to get off his symbolic crack pipe and go back to class.

[Laughter]

Dickerson: It troubles me that we have a brother like this saying things he knows will play to a base, that's all it is. He's offering up tom turkey with all this white meat.

Shipp: Watch it now. No crazy uncles in this room.

Dickerson: Let's call it like it is.

. . .

The train was clackety-clacking at a nice pace. I put my head back on the seat and closed my eyes. Started to drift. My mother told me once that I'd been a fussy child. When I'd get out of control she'd put me in a baby car seat and put the seat on top of the washing machine, and the vibration and sound would lull me to sleep.

Still works.

But one thing a fussy child doesn't like is getting woken up. It can lead to gnarly things.

The voice that pulled me out of slumber was saying, "Sir."

I opened my eyes with malice.

He was either a twenty-year-old who looked fifteen, or a fifteen-year-old who wanted to start shaving. His hair was blond and cut short, military style. He wore a white T-shirt, the sleeves of which hung mostly empty around his spindly arms.

He was holding a pamphlet in his hand, so I could see the front. It had a cartoon drawing on it, a family of four—dad, mom, little boy, and girl—huddling outside their home, looks of fear on their faces. The headline said: Are You Ready for What's Coming?

"Not interested," I said.

"I think you should be," Spindly Arms said.

"What you think doesn't matter to me."

"What's that say on your arm?"

He was looking at my left forearm tat.

"Vincit Omnia Veritas," I said.

Spindly squinted.

"It's Latin," I said. "It means, 'Leave me alone, I'm trying to sleep.'"

He smiled. "Does not. It's something about truth, right?"

That immediately made him more interesting. I snatched

the pamphlet. It was a tri-fold. I opened to the first panel and ran my index finger down the page.

"What are you doing?" Spindly said.

"Sh," I said. I read the next two panels the same way. It took about five seconds. It was a screed against blacks and gays, and warned about a coming domestic war.

"What do you intend to accomplish with this?" I said.

"Knowledge," Spindly said. "People need to wake up."

"There's no knowledge here," I said. "Only rhetoric intended to inflame."

"So what? Are you ready to deal with the facts?"

"I didn't see any facts in here."

"You're just blind, then," Spindly said.

"Sit down," I said.

"Why?"

"Because I want to rest my neck, and because you need to hear a few things."

He sat in the chair opposite me. "*You* need to hear, my friend. They are going to come gunning for you. Anybody who is white. It won't matter."

"So your answer is hate?"

"It's not hate to tell the truth," he said. "The truth will set you free."

"You're quoting Jesus now?" I said.

"You better believe it," he said.

I turned the pamphlet to the back and saw, in small print at the bottom, the name of a church.

"This your church?" I said, holding it up.

"So?"

"You're doing all this in the name of Jesus?"

"That's right. Are you a Christian?"

"More of a blend," I said. "Eighty percent Stoic, fifteen percent Platonic—"

"You're a pagan."

"Now listen, junior. Jesus did not say, 'Go into all the world and call people names.' He said love your neighbor as yourself—"

"You can't quote Jesus—"

"He said love your enemies and do good to those who persecute you."

I was doing pretty good for a guy who'd read the Bible through twice, the last time ten years ago. Of all the philosophical and moral systems out there, it seems to me you can't improve on the Ten Commandments and the Sermon on the Mount. The trick is to get people to buy in. Especially those who claimed to rep him, like Spindly Arms here.

"You don't know anything about Jesus," Spindly said.

"I've read the Sermon on the Mount. And I'm sure Jesus wouldn't talk about people the way you do."

"I know Jesus personally, in my own life."

"You don't know Jesus from a hole in your underwear."

"You're of the devil," he said with absolute conviction.

"I'm more like a baseball announcer," I said.

"I rebuke you!"

"It would be much better if you didn't rebuke anybody and learned to think for yourself. Get away from this claptrap and read some good books."

"God is going to judge you," he said.

"Then I expect he'll be fair," I said.

"He is a God of wrath."

"I got some wrath, too, and if you stay—"

"When this country goes down, you'll pay for it," he said.

"What I paid for is a nice, quiet seat," I said.

"I can stay here if I want to."

"But you don't want to," I said.

He frowned. "Who says?"

"Mr. Peanut," I said.

He kept frowning. I have that effect on people.

There was a small, unopened bag of peanuts on the seat next to me. I picked it up and fastballed it at him. The bag bounced off his chest.

"Hey!" he said. "You threw peanuts at me."

"Now that's a fact," I said. "Go write a pamphlet about it."

For a moment he looked like he wanted to say something else. So I put my hands on the arm rests and feinted like I was going to stand up. That got him up and out of the seat in a hurry, and heading down the aisle.

The whole thing saddened me.

There are three kinds of people in the world. First, there are those who can think, but don't, because it takes work. And they have never been made to work. They've been given inflated grades because self-esteem is more important than actual learning, and their teachers haven't been taught to think, either. So in front of PlayStation the fantasy world bleeds over into the real world and two shall become one flesh.

Then there are those who are told what to think, and take it from whoever moves their loins. It's feelings-based, or some psychosis, as in the case with poor Spindly.

Finally, there are those who actually do think, and who are open to being convinced, should the evidence demand it. This takes work and courage, and those are two of the rarest commodities in any culture, any time.

The first kind of person is a drain.

The second kind is dangerous.

The last kind can end up dead if either of the first two gains power.

Spindly had left his pamphlet. So I decided to do some origami on it. I don't know how to do origami. I crumpled it into a ball, tore some of the paper on either side, and bent those pieces out. And I was done. I had either a blowfish with fins or the head of Prince Charles.

. . .

AS I TRIED once more to get some sleep, a picture popped into my mind. Of a woman named Helen Feist. She was a colleague of my mom's at the Yale Divinity School. When I was ten, my mom was hit with a nasty virus that took her out for a few weeks. This Helen quietly and without fanfare attended to my mom's needs, such as making sure I got to school, and cooking exotic soups that got my mom back on her feet.

Helen Feist walked with a limp. I asked my mom about it and she told me Helen lost her right leg to an infection she got in Calcutta while working with Mother Teresa.

It seems to me that Helen Feist is the picture of Jesus the world ought to see, not the one painted by the guy I'd tagged with peanuts.

The thought calmed me and I started to nod off.

But a pleasant sleep was not to be.

"Sir?"

I opened my eyes. A portly conductor whose head was too big for his hat was standing there. Behind him was a tall man in an ill-fitting gray suit that went with his humorless gray face.

"Sorry to bother you, sir," the conductor said, "but this man says you assaulted his son."

I looked the man in the face. There was a slight resemblance, from the nose to the hate in the eyes.

"Assaulted?" I said.

"You apparently threw an item and hit the son in the chest."

"Oh, you mean the peanuts," I said. "In that case, I salted his son. If his son is afraid of legumes, there's not much I can do."

"I want this man off the train," Gray Suit said.

"Are you kidding?" I said. "Is this the Old West or something?"

"There are rules of conduct, sir," the conductor said.

"Tell you what," I said to Gray Suit, "I'll give your son satis-faction. A duel."

"What?" he said.

"Cashews at ten paces."

"This is outrageous," Gray Suit said. "If he doesn't get off this train I'll press charges."

"Assault with a deadly goober?" I said.

"You think this is funny?"

"Mostly sad," I said. "What are you raising your son to be?"

"I want him off!"

The conductor put his arm up. "If you'll let me handle this, sir. Please."

"I will be checking on you," Gray Suit said, "and with your supervisor."

"I'll take care of it," the conductor said.

The man in the suit gave me a final look, then stormed down the aisle and down the stairs.

I looked at the conductor. He seemed apologetic, but reso-lute. "If he presses this, I'll have to write up an official complaint."

"I could always take him by his pants and throw him off the train," I said.

The conductor tried not to smile. "I'm sorry, sir."

Getting written up in any kind of official capacity was not the way to start off my clandestine operations. I don't think my employers would be pleased.

I said, "I suppose the way to avoid the whole thing is for me to get off the train."

"That would do it, yes."

"Which would be a minor victory for the jerks of this world."

The conductor shrugged.

"And less paperwork for you," I said. "Where's the next stop?"

. . .

TOSSED OFF THE train in San Luis Obispo. I felt like a Greek hero trying to get to Ithaca, now waylaid on the island of lost souls.

This island had a smattering of taxis at the train station. I hailed one. The driver wore a crocheted Persian-style fedora and spoke with an accent.

At least at this moment, the Greeks and the Persians were not at war.

I had him take me to the Greyhound bus station, which turned out to be on the other side of town.

I've been in many Greyhound bus stations. There is a sameness about them, but they each have their own feel, too. With San Luis Obispo midway between L.A. and San Francisco, this place had a stopping-off vibe, a transient feel, a restlessness.

In other words, I fit right in.

I got a bus ticket for San Francisco, the bus leaving in an hour and a half. That gave me time to sit on a hard bench with a vending machine sandwich and my copy of Montaigne.

Life of the party, that's me.

But the time went by and the bus took off. It's not anything like a train. But at least this time no one bothered me. The seat next to me stayed empty.

IT WAS PAST ten when the lights of the city came into view. San Francisco is packed together on hills, a sparkling pincushion of a city. Looked nice on the outside, but there were sharp points underneath.

Steadman had booked me a room at a hotel off Market Street.

It was a bracing night so I decided to walk. I had a single duffel bag with a strap. I did some curls with it as I went. I'm of the Charles Atlas school of getting fit. Atlas gained fame in the early twentieth century as "the worlds' most perfectly developed man." He got together with a business partner and sold a course through the mail. The course was advertised in the back of comic books, with a comic of its own. A skinny guy getting sand kicked in his face by a big bully at the beach. Back home he kicks a chair, crying out how tired he is of getting shamed in front of girls. So he sends for the course and in no time he's buff, goes back to the beach, and punches the bully in the snout. His girl now loves him because he's become a real man.

Such is the hagiography of the American male.

But when you cut through it, Atlas was basically touting a series of isometrics. He'd seen lions at the zoo exercising their own muscles that way.

It works. So even if you're walking in San Francisco at night with a bag, you can give your muscles something to do.

And deep breathing. Charles Atlas liked that, too. It's good for you. So I did, and the smell of ocean and fish mixed with the scent of cars and cables. I walked through the Embarcadero and then up Pine, and right on Kearny. Off in the distance Coit Tower was lit up like a glow stick. I turned again onto a street that was narrow and where the signs had more Chinese script. I checked the address of the hotel once more, and knew I was getting close. I thought about stopping at an all-nighter and having something to eat.

I stopped for a second and checked my phone. No messages.

The moment I put the phone back in my pocket I got shoved from behind, into a wall. Barely got my hand up in time to keep my face from making an impression. I dropped my bag and did a one-eighty, crouching, ready to strike. There were two guys standing there, one of them holding a knife.

"Put your wallet on the ground," the knife-wielder said. He

was the taller of the two, and skinny. His hair was not exactly what you'd call finely coiffed. It was stringy, is what it was, hanging to his shoulders.

"Look, guys, I'm just visiting," I said.

They were in their twenties, white. The other guy was shorter and stockier. Maybe fat if the light was better. He took out a telescopic steel baton and triggered it out. "I'm gonna break your legs," he said.

"This is not cricket," I said.

They looked at each other. I could have taken them both out then, but I was feeling compassionate.

"I'll let you go," I said.

"You hear that?" Knife Guy said. "He's gonna let us go."

Baton Guy smiled. Before he took a step, I calculated the geometric pattern he'd take to get into striking position. He would have to pull the baton back, too, which would buy me another few fractions of a second.

My timing was perfect, and I knew Baton Guy had never listened in Geometry class. The moment he took the baton back I dropped the way a soccer player does when he kicks the ball back over his head. What I kicked was two balls.

Baton Guy doubled over into a perfect right angle.

I anticipated Knife Guy's move, which was to come directly at me in my prone position. But he was slow and I grabbed Baton Guy's shirt and pulled him down, a human shield.

Again, timing perfect. I could feel the knife go into Baton Guy's side.

Poor Baton Guy was having a bad night.

I pushed him away from me, rolled right and sprang to my feet. Knife Guy looked like he was in a horror movie and just saw the monster behind the door.

He started running.

I caught him within twenty yards by the back of his shirt. I cupped my free hand and banged him on the ear. That little move creates instant disequilibrium. Dragging him back to his fallen comrade was no problem.

Baton Guy was groaning and holding his side. A good amount of blood was already on the ground.

I threw Knife Guy on top of him, crosswise, so they formed a plus sign. I put my foot on Knife Guy's back and pressed.

Baton Guy shrieked.

"I don't want anybody bleeding to death, okay?" I said. "I think your problem is education. There's just no discipline anymore. You have to know there are consequences for bad behavior. Without that, society falls apart."

Baton Guy croaked, "I can't breathe."

"You just can't go around doing this sort of thing," I said. "It isn't right. Now, one of you is bleeding pretty badly and won't be riding a bike anytime soon. The other one still needs to learn, am I right?"

"Don't kill us," Knife Guy said.

"I'm not a murderer," I said. "But if you two keep this up you're going to come to a bad end. What I want you to do is go to a library and check out a book. Will you do that for me?"

"I can't breathe!"

"The book is the Bible. I want you to find the Sermon on the Mount in there. Okay? Say, Sermon on the Mount."

Neither one said anything, so I pulled Knife Guy's arm behind him and bent it to the breaking point. He screamed.

"Say Sermon on the Mount," I said.

He didn't, so I bent his arm some more. Then he squealed something that sounded like Sermon on the Mount, like a two-year old was saying it.

"Read that and think about it, right?"

Knife Guy didn't need any further prodding and nodded his head.

"Good," I said. "Now I just have to emphasize this with a consequence for your bad behavior. Hang on." I took hold of Knife Guy's right index finger and bent it back until it cracked.

He screamed.

Baton Guy had grown silent.

I pulled Knife Guy off and laid him down next to his partner. He had a wallet in the back of his pants. I took it. I rolled Baton Guy over. He was almost out. He had a wallet, too. I took it.

"I'm going to call for an ambulance now. I wouldn't try to get away. You're bleeding too much. You'll get taken care of. I'll make sure to follow your progress. If I feel you haven't learned a lesson here tonight, I'll find you. I know your names. I'll be like an angel, okay? You do bad things, I'll know it. And I'll pay you a visit."

I stood. If anyone had seen the commotion in the alley, they did the standard urban thing and ignored it.

"You two have been given a great gift tonight," I said.

With that I grabbed my duffel bag and walked out of the alley. I walked with my head down for a block, then another. I called 911 and made my voice sound like Cary Grant. I reported what looked like a bleeding man and gave the location of the alley and then signed off.

I doubted the cops would find the two guys. They would do what it took to get away from there. I really hoped Baton Guy wouldn't die. Everybody should read the Sermon on the Mount at least once before they die.

THE HOTEL WAS called The Serene and it looked like it was built in 1930 by the Salvation Army. Inside the tiled lobby, behind a Plexiglas window, sat a combover with a man underneath it. His scanty hairs were fighting his forehead like a last bastion of guerrillas in the hills. The end of the war was near.

I gave him my name and he told me the bill was taken care of, pay-as-you-go with someone already paying, and wasn't that a good deal for me? He slipped an old-fashioned key with a green plastic fob into a metal tray and shot the tray out to me.

I asked him how late room service was open and he didn't smile. This place needed a sense of humor to go with its end-of-the-line look. But clearly it wasn't going to be found here at the desk. And not in the empty lobby, where some old chairs waited for desperate butts to give them warmth in the morning.

I got to my room on the second floor with a view of the blank wall next door. The faceless, windowless building squeezed up tight against my room. If I pressed my face against the glass, I got a crack of a street view.

Closing the curtains, I mumbled a line from Epictetus. *Make thou the best of use of what is within thy power, and take the rest as it happens.*

You got it, Epic. I tossed the two wallets on the bed and made an inspection. After a couple of minutes I took out the pre-prepped phone Steadman had given me and called Ira. In addition to being an ex-Mossad assassin and current avuncular rabbi, Ira Rosen is one of the great computer geeks with connections to Israel and U.S. intel. He is handier than Google and smarter than the NSA.

"Ira."

"Mike! How's the city by the bay?"

"Unfriendly," I said. "I got jumped by a couple of guys."

"You're kidding, right?"

"Not kidding. One had a knife and one had a club. I had to hurt them."

"Oh no."

"I took their wallets."

"Oh no, no."

"It's okay. They may have made it to a hospital."

"May have?"

"I wasn't going to drive them, Ira."

"How bad was it?"

"One guy lost a lot of blood."

"Oh no."

"But here's the good news——"

"There's good news?"

"Yes, there's a nice little sandwich shop right outside the hotel."

Silence.

"Ira?"

"I'm here. God help me, I'm here."

"Let me give you their names. You can run them for me."

"Why?"

"For informational purposes. You never know."

"You never know what?"

"I can't tell you that. That's what *you never know* means."

He sighed. "Okay, give me the names."

"Neil Smoltz is one, and Gavin Thomas is the other. They both live in Walnut Creek." I gave him the addresses.

"Anything else I need to know?" Ira said.

"Things can only get better from here," I said. "Or worse."

"You know, Romeo, sometimes your philosophical musings seem like complete nonsense."

"It's a gift."

I cut off the call and took off my shoes and looked around the room and thought this would be a good place to be a monk with a vow of silence and one hard-boiled egg for breakfast every morning. I pulled one of the books Sophie had saved for me, the volume on Thomas Reid, and it brought good thoughts of her again. I stripped down and propped myself up and read Scottish common sense realism for about half an hour, then fell asleep. I dreamed that life was logical and made sense.

A scream woke me up.

My own.

I'D BEEN DREAMING of chestnuts roasting on the streets of New York, at night, during Christmas. A smell I always loved. Even better than the eating. In the dream the chestnuts were roasting on my shoulder. But I was only eight, a kid again, and my father was standing next to me, in his big black over-coat and the fedora he loved, the black one with the black ribbon. The library was all lit up, the one on 42nd Street, the place I always went when my dad or mom brought me into the city. And the chestnuts were burning, burning, and then they popped, popped loud, not like chestnuts but like gunfire, and my father went down with holes in him and that's when I screamed and woke up.

I do that once every six months or so.

Then I stare into the darkness until my heart slows down and my breathing gets normal, and if I'm lucky, I fall back asleep.

IN THE MORNING I showered in water the color of Seabis-cuit's doping sample. At seven-thirty I left my elegant hotel and walked in the morning gloom to Columbus Avenue and the place Steadman told me I'd find Katarina Hogg.

She was there. The face was unmistakable. It was framed by shoulder-length chestnut hair parted on the left side with a little curling action under the chin. She wore a brown, pinstriped suit over an open-collar black blouse.

She also had a neon *Do Not Disturb* sign on her forehead as she studied a tablet propped at an angle in front of her. A large-sized white cup with a brown heat sleeve was on the left side. A southpaw. That was good to know. Lefties are quirky. You can play to their quirks.

I was dressed like a lawyer on vacation—khaki pants, pale-blue Oxford shirt, slip-on brown shoes. A pro costume.

"Ms. Hogg?"

She snapped me a look. She had a tight, unsmiling face that was not unfriendly. It was rigid with the cool impatience of the interrupted professional. It would have taken a blowtorch to defrost those lips so the teeth could come out for a laugh.

"Yes?" she said, clipped, as if every word she said was going to be deducted from a time sheet.

"I understand your campaign is looking for some security."

She sat back, looked me up and down, back at my face. She could have been a federal meat inspector.

"We have an office for that," she said.

"I thought you might like to see that I can find somebody if need be. And I figured it would save us both time."

More inspection. "Just how did you find me?"

"It wasn't hard," I said. "Photos on the net, and an article said you like to work here."

She locked her eyes on mine. It was a look intended to secure the high ground, like Buford at Gettysburg. She was making it clear who was in control. "It's kind of creepy, actually."

I recalled my Sun Tzu. *If your enemy has superior strength, pretend to be weak, that he may grow arrogant.* "You're right," I said.

She raised her eyebrows.

I said, "But once you get to know me, I'm only disturbing."

The mouth defrosted for a moment and one corner of it curved up.

She gestured to the opposite chair. I sat.

She put her elbows on the table and clasped her hands together, looking at me over her tablet. "Name?" she said.

"Mike Romeo."

"Experience?"

"Ten years."

"References?"

"One," I said.

"That's not very many."

"The rest are confidential."

"I'm supposed to take your word for that?"

"Yes," I said.

She picked up her coffee and put it to her lips. She sipped, her eyes never leaving mine. "Why us?"

"I'm looking for work and I'm good at what I do."

"What's your party affiliation?"

"None."

"You're not registered voter?"

"No."

"Why not?"

"I don't like being registered by anybody."

"That's quite an attitude," she said.

"It started in nursery school," I said. "I wanted to schedule my own naps."

Both sides of her mouth curved up. I was flanking my way up the high ground.

Kat Hogg looked at her tablet and tapped the index finger of her right hand on the table. Finally, she said, "You'd better go through the application process."

There are times when you're in a cage when the decision has to be made without analysis. You just hope that all your training and experience pays off when it needs to. Kat Hogg was trying to get me off balance, and I had to determine if she had a good stance or was wobbly herself.

I chose wobbly.

"No thanks," I said. "I'll look elsewhere. Nice meeting you."

I got up from the table, gave her a nod, turned my back. I calculated that three steps would mean I was cooked, that I'd failed, that I'd head back to L.A. and tell them the whole plan was in the dumper. But thanks for the trip to Frisco.

But when I took the second step, Kat Hogg said, "Wait a second."

I turned.

"Let me ask you a question," she said. She nodded at the chair and I sat.

"Have you heard of Father Dwayne Weaver?" she asked.

"Sure."

"Like him?"

"What's not to like?" I said. In reality, I'd seen him on news clips once or twice and thought he was a loud-talking faker, a religious charlatan and an untrustworthy hack. Not that I had a strong opinion or anything.

"Do you ever think he's over the top?"

"In what way?"

"The words he says, the way he says them?"

I sensed a trap. But I also sensed part of her harbored a small whiff of doubt about the man she was describing.

"If you believe something," I said, "you should say it with conviction. But you should also be able to back it up."

"Back it up how?"

"With principles, facts and logic."

She shook her head slightly. "You're interesting," she said.

"I've been called worse," I said.

"Okay," she said. "I want you to meet somebody."

"JAY J. PARSONS, I'd like you to meet Mike Romeo."

Parsons stood and offered his hand. His expression was wary, but I figured that went with his territory. The hair he had left on his head was sandy-colored, mixed with oncoming gray. His eyebrows and trimmed beard were almost all white. He looked like he kept himself in shape. There was a mountain bike leaning against the wall of his office.

"When Kat brings a recommendation, that's pretty high praise," he said.

"We can all use a little praise now and then," I said.

He motioned for us to sit. Through the glass windows of his office I could see worker bees at desks, doing various things —stuffing envelopes, scanning tablets, talking on phones. A large, framed portrait of Genevieve Griffin smiled from a square pillar in the middle of things. Big Sister looking down on a campaign in full swing.

"What are you known for, Mike?" he said.

"Excuse me?" I said.

"Everybody's known for something. Take me. You know what I'm known for?"

"I can't say that I do."

"I'm known for my powers of persuasion. I used to be in sales. And you know what they used to say about me?"

"I really can't say that I do."

"They used to say I could have sold brass knuckles to Gandhi."

Kat smiled. So did Parsons.

Parsons said, "So what is your thing, Mike? The thing that you are known for among the people who know you."

"That's not a big circle," I said. "But I suppose you could say it's that I do what needs to be done. I protect who needs to be protected."

Parsons picked up a letter opener, put the point on his index finger, and twirled it. "Who've you worked for?"

"Confidential," I said.

"Except one," Kat said. "I've got it."

Parsons studied me a moment. "You can keep confidences then?"

"It goes with the job."

He nodded. "I have a job to do, too. My job is to run a smooth campaign and use only trustworthy people. What makes you trustworthy, Mike? I mean, for example, can you do what you're told?"

No.

"Yes." I took a method acting class once, when I was sixteen. My mom thought it would be good for expanding my social skills, which were not exactly well developed. But I loved that class. It was taught by a disciple of Stella Adler. And I learned that's what acting is, being able to lie convincingly. The way you did it was adopt something of your own life and mold it like Silly Putty into the life you were creating for the character. I learned from that class how to look someone in the eye and speak with conviction.

As I was doing now with Jay J. Parsons. I was playing the part of Mike Romeo, trustworthy taker of orders. Brando would have been proud.

Kat said, "I can run the regular background, Jay J. And we can use the balance."

Parsons nodded. "One of the things a guy in my position has to do is keep everybody happy. It may surprise you to know that not everybody in this world is happy."

"Valle lacrimarum," I said.

"What's that?"

"Sounds like Latin," Kat said.

"Vale of tears," I said. "One description of life."

Parsons tapped his bearded chin with the letter opener. "You interest me, Mike. Where'd you go to school?"

"I'm mostly self-taught," I said.

Kat was smiling. She seemed to be enjoying whatever this was.

Parsons said, "The security detail for Father Dwayne Weaver is always handled by Shipp's crowd. You know who I'm talking about?"

"Of course," I said. Everybody knew about the Reverend Rodney Shipp and his crew. He considered himself a marked man.

Parsons said, "He has his own detail, the military look and all. I'm sure you've seen that on Fox News."

"I don't watch Fox News."

"I like you already."

"So what's this about balance?"

"It's a touchy subject, so we'll just keep it simple. This is supposed to be a rally for Genevieve Griffin. I mean, she's the one running for reelection."

"Will she be there?"

"Not till later. For security purposes. It'll be a surprise. But when you get Shipp and Weaver together, there's a rivalry. Shipp tends to try to dominate things wherever he goes. Sometimes that's good, but other times, well ..."

"You don't want any bad Shipp happening."

Parsons blinked. Kat smiled.

Parsons said, "He's a great man, a legend, but he's been saying some things we wish he wouldn't say. And if his security team is the one that's seen all over the place, it'll just feed into that narrative of his being, you know, dangerous to white folks. So we're trying to balance the racial makeup of the security team. Make sense?"

"Image is everything," I said.

"Pretty close," Parsons said.

"So this will be a good tryout," Kat said.

Parsons leaned back in his chair, looked at the ceiling and fiddled with the letter opener.

I looked at Kat. She winked at me. I hadn't had a good wink thrown my way in a long time. I liked it.

Parsons swung back and said, "Mike, I wonder if you might give Kat and me a moment?"

"Sure," I said.

Outside the office, I listened to the hum of activity and watched the volunteers. I wondered how many of them were true believers and how many had challenged themselves to think about what they were doing, and why.

One figure by the window looked out of place. Not because of her physicality, which was San Francisco friendly. She had dark, black eye shadow, blackened hair without shine, and tattoos snaking under a black tank top. If I had to guess, I would have said she was into black. One of her ears was a stud garden. There was more silver than flesh showing.

She was stuffing envelopes.

Then she looked at me. Her eyes were like an abandoned building. The lights had been on once, but now the electricity was shut off.

She flipped me the bird.

I guess that's how you win elections in California.

Kat called my name. I went back into the office.

"Congratulations," Jay J. Parsons said. "Subject to the normal background check, you've to the job. Kat will fill you in."

First step accomplished. In with Kat Hogg and on the periphery of the campaign. If I wasn't yet in the belly of the beast, I could at least now smell its breath.

AN HOUR LATER, Kat was driving us in her red Subaru across the Bay Bridge toward Oakland. About which Gertrude Stein once said, There is no there there.

But at least there was a reason for me going. Part of the prep for my muscle job. And that meant meeting with the security team, the one Parsons was worried would turn off grandmothers in Orange County.

"Shipp is smart," Kat said. "He doesn't want them to have a

formal name. He doesn't want some news hound calling them the New Black Panthers."

"There's already a New Black Panthers."

"I suppose they could be Newer. Or Fresher. Whatever, he doesn't want that. Just between you and me, they like to call themselves the Dogs of War. They do have a structure, and Kwame is the lead guy."

"Kwame?"

"Yeah. Just Kwame. He takes a little getting used to. In Kindergarten he probably got a 'Does not play well with others.' "

I glanced left and could see the top of Alcatraz. The perfect spot once for all the guys who did not play well with others.

"So why are you even messing around with him?" I said. "Does Genevieve Griffin have anything to do with this?"

"It's a delicate relationship," Kat said. "Between Shipp and Weaver, and Genevieve. She is the kind of person who wants everybody to be happy. She's tough as iron, don't get me wrong. You don't ever want to get on her bad side. But she also would rather have people just get along."

"In the land of unicorns and rainbows," I said.

Kat laughed. "I'm not even sure why I'm driving with you."

"To get me to Oakland."

"Your involvement is moving faster than normal."

"You can pull the plug if you want."

"I'm willing to give this a shot. Maybe you can save me a few steps. Where were you born?"

New York.

"St. Louis," I said. "I went to college but dropped out and went traveling around. My *On the Road* phase."

"What did you learn?"

"I learned how to eat." That much was true. "I learned to figure out who you could trust."

"Can you trust me?"

"I don't know," I said.

"At least you're honest," she said.

"Tell me about *your* background," I said.

She didn't answer right away. I tapped my fingernails on the window glass.

"I'm a farm girl," she said. "From Kansas. Just like Dorothy."

"You're a long way from home."

"In a lot of ways," she said.

"Explain."

"I don't want to bore you."

"No life is boring if you drill down far enough."

She shook her head. "Maybe someday."

"Tell me why Genevieve Griffin is so afraid of Samuel Johnson."

"He's mounting a challenge," she said. "Isn't that enough?"

"How close is he?"

"Close enough that we can't take a chance on being complacent."

"Griffin's been in office a long time. Her favorables are pretty good, aren't they?"

"They've slipped a little. You never know, especially when the economy's doing a dive. A lot of things could come together and create a perfect storm."

I dangled some bait in the water. "This personal thing's going to hurt Johnson."

"What personal thing?"

"Isn't there something about a woman he had a thing with?"

She paused. "What do you know about it?"

"Nothing. Internet gossip. There's some sort of blog dedicated to the rumors, isn't there?"

"I don't really know," she said.

"It's easy to start a rumor," I said.

And then we almost rammed into the car ahead of us. Kat hit the brakes hard. The car behind us honked like a mad goose.

"I can see I'm not helping you drive," I said.

"I'm much better than I appear," she said.

I wondered if that was true.

WE HEADED INTO the tunnel. I looked at her dashboard, her shoes, her legs, the floorboard under my feet. Everything about the car and Katarina Hogg was sleek, functional and, in parts, beautiful.

And suddenly I felt out of place, like a pair of black socks with sandals. I just hoped it didn't show.

When we got out of the tunnel there was Oakland, beckoning, if Oakland can ever be said to beckon. Ten minutes later, we were driving through parts that people tend to avoid unless they live there.

Kat did not seem uneasy. Even when she got to a fenced-off parking lot and drove up the gate, she was perfectly relaxed. I admired that.

A black man in fatigues and sunglasses and not looking like a kindly old gentleman stepped out from under an umbrella. He had a belt with security things hanging on it, including a holstered weapon. From the look and thickness of the butt, I figured it was a Taser with an air cartridge.

Kat gave him a half wave. He unlocked the gate and rolled it open. He did not nod or smile or wave. We drove inside and parked next to a motorcycle. We were in front of a commercial building, painted black with a blood-red symbol over the entrance. The symbol was a pit bull baring its teeth and curled around into the shape of a circle.

We got out and went to the doors, where another

uniformed guy met us. He had shades, too, and was in a stink-look contest with the first guy.

Kat led me down the corridor, which was lit by bare light bulbs. There were double doors at the end of the corridor, and this time Kat pushed it open herself. I followed her into a large chamber that might have once been for storage. But there were no shelves, no racks, no forklifts.

But there was gym equipment. A weight station, a heavy bag for boxing, a basketball hoop. A couple of guys were lifting, their exhalations echoing through the place.

The clang of weights stopped and one of the men who had been bench pressing sat up. His stare across the floor was heat-seeking. He reached for sunglasses and put them on, then walked across the floor.

Kat gave him a nod which he did not return.

"Kwame, this is Mike," she said.

I put my hand out. He didn't shake it. I couldn't see his eyes behind the shades.

"Mike's going to help us with security tomorrow night," she said.

"Don't need no help," Kwame said.

There was something familiar about him.

"Jay J wants him there," Kat said.

"Jay J can kiss my—"

"Kwame, you work for us on this one."

"You don't tell me who I work for," Kwame said.

What was it I saw in him? The shape of his body, the cut of his face.

Then I had it. "Hey, you're Kwame Owens," I said.

His frozen face didn't crack. "Don't use that name now."

"You had a couple great seasons with the Lions."

"That's all over."

"I saw your pick six against against Green Bay in the play-offs. It was a thing of beauty."

"Told you, no more of that. I ain't no meat on the hoof."

"We're cooperating this time," Kat said. "Shipp answers to Jay J on this one."

"How come?" Kwame said.

"Because he doesn't want any cameras picking up you guys outside, and then it's blasted all over Fox for the next ten years."

Kwame's smile oozed contempt. "So white folks got to be outside, black folks inside in the broom closet."

"Kwame," Kat said, "you are so 1965."

I had to admire her. She wasn't taking anything from the football player turned paramilitary intimidator.

He turned to me. "I'm the onsite go-to. You do what you're told and shut up."

"Got it," I said.

"You don't talk 'less you talked to."

I nodded.

"You don't talk to any of my boys."

I did not say anything.

"I see you inside, that's the last time I'm gonna see you."

"How much longer is this going to go on?" I said.

He stepped up to my face. "Long as I want. You got a problem with that?"

"Not as much of a problem as I do with Hegel, but yeah."

Kwame looked at Kat. "Who's he talking about?"

"No idea," Kat said. Then to me, "Who are you talking about?"

"Friederich Hegel," I said. "Dialectical materialism."

That unsnapped a few invisible vest buttons on Kwame. He got eye-to-eye with me again, and I could now see his orbs through the dark glass of his shades. They were taking a bead on me like the D-back he once was, homing in on a defenseless receiver. I recalled that Kwame Owens had been suspended one season for a series of head shots, one of which ended another player's career.

"That's the first and last time you try to show me up," Kwame said, in a way that invited response.

My fists wanted to get in on the action, but my brain knocked on my skull and reminded me I wasn't here representing myself.

"No problem," I said.

Kwame moved his head around a little, the way a goose does before it pecks at a rival.

"Not here," Kwame said. "Not now. But someday we gonna have private talk. 'Less you get out of town."

"Not until I pick up some sourdough bread," I said.

"Do you two idiots know you're on the same team?" Kat said.

"Ain't on my team," Kwame said.

"Tomorrow night he is," Kat said.

Kwame looked at her. "If he stays out the way."

"Don't upset the Shipp," Kat said.

I tried not to laugh, but it was close. To cover myself I said to Kwame, "Let's give it a shot. I won't get in your way. I'll do my job and get out."

I stuck out my hand.

Again, he didn't take it.

"That's right," Kwame said.

"WELL THAT WAS a delight," I said as we drove back across the bridge.

"Isn't he just the consummate gentleman?" Kat said.

She laughed and it was nice, and then she drove for a while in silence. I listened to the hum of the cars on the bridge. Alcatraz was to the right of me, Kat to the left of me, forward the light brigade.

The Rock—notorious federal pen, enclave of the walking dead. Last stop. Isolation. Kiss tomorrow good-bye.

Katarina Hogg—educated, competent, professional, beautiful. Promise, ambition, sky's the limit. Who does she kiss?

Romeo in the middle, looking at it all with jaundiced eye, kissing nobody.

Kat said, "How about some dinner tonight on the campaign's dime?"

"You're taking me out to dinner?"

"The *campaign*. Consider it part of the interview process. Where you staying?"

"A luxury hotel. If the bedbugs don't eat you, it's a luxury."

She smiled. "I'll pick you up at seven."

"I'll meet you at the corner. It's safer."

MY LUXURY HOTEL didn't have Wi-Fi, so I took the iPad Steadman gave me and plopped myself at a Starbucks on Mission.

I did a little more research on Katarina Hogg. She was quoted in several stories as a spokesperson for the Griffin campaign. A lot of typical spin. There was a profile of her in *The Hoya,* Georgetown University's student newspaper, from several years ago. She was interviewed after landing a job with Genevieve Griffin's DC staff.

With a smile, Hogg cites her "evolution" into political awareness as beginning in Fr. Frank Jameson's class in Activist Literature. "I came from a homeschool program where we learned evolution was evil," she says. "To say that I've evolved into anything would be a scandal back home."

. . .

The piece went on to describe Kat Hogg as having a less-than-exciting social life ("No time!"). Genevieve Griffin was quoted as saying, "Kat is one of the most dynamic young aides I've seen come around this town in a long time. The sky's the limit for her."

So far, everything about Katarina Hogg seemed polished and professional. I looked at images of her and there were mostly publicity shots. Kat looked like a model in a couple of them. There was one candid shot of Jay J. Parsons coming out of a restaurant, smiling and waving. On his right arm was Kat Hogg. She was looking at the ground, without a smile.

I switched over to searching Kwame Owens. There was a lot of stuff from his NFL days, of course. Once Kwame Owens became a starter for the Lions, he began a career that might have put him in the Hall of Fame. His hits were vicious. And Owens loved his rep as an assassin. He even said he was proud that the league began to change its rules because of the hit he laid on Raiders wide receiver Delroy McQueen in a game in Oakland. It was from behind, just before the ball reached McQueen's outstretched hands. McQueen had jumped and was completely helpless.

The sound of the hit, some said, could be heard across the bay.

Delroy McQueen did not get up. They came out with a stretcher, had to secure his head so it wouldn't move. Later, they told Delroy McQueen he would never walk again. When Kwame heard that from a teammate he infamously said, "What's one less Raider?" Oh, how the newspapers and TV reporters attacked that. They came after Owens with a bunch of microphones in the locker room the next Sunday. Kwame Owens faced them calmly. "That's football, man," he said. "That's the game. It was a clean hit. What am I gonna do? Ain't gonna change the way I play the game."

So the suits in the league office went to work on the rule

book. And Kwame Owens started getting called "the dirtiest player in the game." Every indication was he wore it like a badge of honor. He never went to see Delroy McQueen. He never apologized for the hit.

A famous video interview he did with sports commentator Jim Rome was on YouTube, with well over three million hits. In the in-studio interview Rome was aggressively questioning Owens about his play, his leading the league in penalties, and a recent two-game suspension. At one point Kwame tells Rome to back off. Rome tells him to chill.

Next thing, Kwame is on his feet, grabbing Rome by his tie and almost lifting the host into a hanging position. Rome's eyes pop wide open, and then a couple of his TV crew get in there and start to pull Kwame off him. Kwame turns around and throws one of the guys off the little platform. A headset goes flying. Then the picture cuts off.

If you get a rep like Owens, there's always a big chance there'll be retaliation. Two years after putting Delroy McQueen in a wheelchair for life, Kwame Owens got gang tackled by karma in New Orleans. A couple of Saints went for his knees, and there was a rumor they had it planned, the whole team. A play designed to Kwame's side of the field just so the tight end could cross-block him low. Kwame later claimed they'd put a bounty out on him, but nobody talked, nobody ever proved anything. The league investigated but not, it seemed, with a lot of enthusiasm.

That hit tore up Kwame's ACL, and that was that. Kwame Owens tried to come back two years later, but he couldn't do the lateral moves anymore. He'd lost a step-and-a-half of speed. It was over.

I next looked at a story about his life after football. The title of it was *Kwame Owens: Unrepentant and Unstoppable.* It had a picture of him without his shirt, taken from a low angle. He had his arms crossed and he glared down at the camera. The story was about how he was going into the food services business.

A story a year later profiled Kwame (he had dropped the Owens, he said, because it represented slave ownership) and said he was dedicating his life to "putting the hurt" on systemic racism in America. He was being mentored by no less than Dr. Rodney Shipp himself.

Further in-depth stories about Kwame dried up after that.

But there was one last hit that intrigued me. It was an interview Delroy McQueen had given to *Sports Illustrated* a few years back. He was still living in Oakland, had gone to seminary, and was an assistant pastor at a Baptist church. Working with the kids in the community on character and sports. Naturally they asked him about Kwame Owens and the hit that put him in a wheelchair for life. "I forgave him long ago," McQueen was quoted as saying. "I've found peace with God through my Lord Jesus Christ, and I pray every day that Kwame Owens might find the same thing."

Peace. God. What did all that really mean? My mother was the spiritual one in the family. My dad believed Aquinas proved the existence of an uncaused cause, but that you couldn't go beyond that. My mom told him that was nonsense, that personality was evident in the things created, in beauty, in music, in love. I sat listening to them at the dinner table, Vivaldi playing in the background, and they would put me in the conversation, and I tried to sound as smart as they were.

And now here we are in Starbucks in San Francisco, and all this fever about politics and dirty tricks and muggings on the street and what good is anything going to do anybody in one hundred years?

Good thing I hadn't been hired to write speeches.

When I'd had enough of the research and the musings, I called Steadman and filled him in on meeting Kat Hogg and Jay J. Parsons.

"What did you think of Jay J?" Steadman asked me with a giddy excitement.

I said, "Sort of a laid back NorCal kind of guy, but with Washington-insider duplicity."

Pause. "Yeah. Exactly! I've known him a long time, and that's exactly right. So what else?"

"I got a security job. Tomorrow night. Father Dwayne Weaver is holding a rally. Rodney Shipp's going to be there."

"That's amazing you got that!"

"I'm just an amazing guy."

"Anything else?"

"You know anything about Shipp's paramilitary crew?"

"Oh yeah," Steadman said. "The Dogs or something like that. The news orgs don't give a flying rip what they do, so it's pointless to make them an issue."

"They have a head guy who is trouble on steroids."

"Yeah, Koomie or something like that."

"Something like that."

"Steer clear of them," Steadman said.

"They're part of the security detail. They're running things."

"Unbelievable."

"I'll see if I can find something you can run with."

"Like what?"

"I won't know it until I see it," I said. "But I think I can guarantee it'll show up."

"Mike?"

"Yeah?"

"Be careful."

"You kidding? If I was careful I'd be sipping suds in Sarasota."

"You come up with the craziest things," Steadman said. "I love it."

.   .   .

THE RESTAURANT OVERLOOKED Fisherman's Wharf and had an old sea-faring interior design. But the clientele was strictly upper deck. My lawyer-on-vacation look was just right.

Kat knew the maitre'd and called him Carl. He smiled at her then eyed me like a ship's captain sizing up a deckhand.

We got a booth on the second level, the horseshoe bench seating facing a large window. Out the window was a view of old-school San Francisco mixed with tourist traffic. We could see the crab stands in the shadow of *Alioto's*, steam rising from pots, a large woman in Oklahoma clothes pointing her camera phone at a man in a white apron holding up a big crab in both hands, and from there, a direct line out to that self-same Rock that had me so reflective earlier that day. There was something about it now that was Stephen Kingish—like it was a malevolent presence rising out of the sea, heading for land, hungry for souls.

A waiter, looking like a model doing time in the service industry, gave us his introductory song and dance, told us about a special involving mahi-mahi and Macadamia nuts, and asked us if we'd like something from the bar. Kat asked to see the wine list, and I sat back to watch her take control of the dinner.

That's what she wanted. To establish the pecking order. I'd let her peck. She was picking up the tab after all.

"You like the place?" she said.

"Pretty generous of you."

"You'll find we are very generous with the people who work for us."

"Do I work for you?"

"Maybe."

"What's the pay?"

"I'll work up an offer."

"When?"

"After dessert." She smiled. She was good at it.

The waiter came back with the leather-bound list and Kat reached for it. "May I select a wine?"

"By all means," I said.

"Something red and robust?"

"As long as it captures a childhood summer in Provence."

"Are you for real?" she said.

"No," I said.

"Good." She scanned the wine list. I looked out the window at the rock monster rising from the sea.

"Rosenthal has a lovely cabernet," Kat said.

"I'm all for it."

I was getting the distinct impression there was nothing Katarina Hogg did without purpose and poise. She was casting her hook and it was just this side of being too obvious.

"You did not look at all afraid of Kwame," she said, setting the wine list on the table.

"Fear is a sliding scale," I said.

"So you were afraid?"

"I'd say I was ready."

She put her elbows on the table and her chin on her hands. "I'm going to ply you with alcohol and get some answers out of you."

"Do your worst," I said.

The waiter came back and Kat ordered the wine. The sun was setting on San Francisco. Lights starting to make their appearance, Alcatraz biding its time with a single illuminated eyeball checking us out.

"Now," she said, "In the interest of full disclosure—"

"What a novel idea."

"—I want you to know I did a little background on you before we went over to Oakland, and it's a very curious thing. You don't have many connections to actual people."

"No man is an island," I said.

"John Donne."

"I'm impressed. What was your major in college?"

"Comparative Lit."

"What's your favorite novel?"

She sat back in her chair. "*Gatsby*."

"I'll take *The Maltese Falcon* over *Gatsby*," I said.

"I've never read *The Maltese Falcon*," she said.

"I can't have dinner with you now."

"I'll read it. I promise."

"Okay, then" I said. "But you're on thin ice."

"Hey, I'm supposed to be asking you the questions."

"The interrogation continues?"

"Don't put it that way," she said. "I do have a job and a responsibility."

"Ask away."

"I CAN ONLY get back so far into your past," she said. "I get back to when you were fighting, but before that there's virtually nothing. There was some fluff of a bio in a program once, but to be quite honest with you, it didn't sound believable."

"That's because it was fiction," I said. "They needed something, so I made something up."

"Okay, then what's the real story?"

"It's not something I choose to publicize."

"And that," she said, "is what interests me."

"I also believe in privacy. What I choose to keep private is nobody's business."

"Which means you have something to hide."

"Everybody has something to hide," I said. "Tell me about your sex life."

Her cheeks flushed, obvious even in the candlelight.

"See?" I said.

"I could get really mad at this point."

"But you won't," I said. "Because it's not a good move. And

my impression of you is that you make nothing but good moves."

Before she could answer, the waiter appeared with the bottle of wine. They went through the ceremony, Kat swirled and smelled and tasted. "Childhood summer," she announced. The waiter filled the glasses.

She told the waiter to come back later.

Raising her glass she said, "To solving mysteries."

"To privacy," I said.

We clinked and drank. The wine was full and complex and pleasing. I found myself wondering if Kat was the same. Or was she all performance?

"Will you at least tell me where you grew up and where you went to school?" Kat said.

"Tell you what," I said. "Let's make an exchange. I'll give a little, and you give a little."

She cocked her head and pointed at me. "Just be careful."

I said, "I grew up in the east, and went to prep school and college. I dropped out of college and went my own way for a while."

"Why did you drop out?"

"Personal reasons. And after being in books all my life, I thought I better see what life was like. I'm still on tour."

"What about your parents? Are they—?"

"Now it's your turn. I want to know why you're in politics."

"Is that so hard to understand?"

"Absolutely."

"Why?"

"Because motives are complex," I said. "Especially when it comes to politics. You could be in it for selfless reasons, or for pure ambition. Or something in between."

"What do you think I'm in it for?" she said.

"Why are you answering a question with a question?" I said.

She lifted her glass to me and we clinked again.

"Is Romeo your real name?"

"Yes."

"Was it always your real name?"

"Before that I was Iago."

"You're not going to let me in, are you?"

"We're circling. We're not dancing."

"Do you ever dance?"

"When the music's right."

It was time to order. We dropped the digging up of the past. It was like a mutual realization that we just didn't want to go there anymore. So we talked about other things. Her interest in history and literature, her love of Fitzgerald and Jane Austen. I talked about Plato and baseball.

Over dinner, as the stars came out to a clear night sky, the subject turned to music and movies. She liked Diana Krall and Madeleine Peyroux, and Sofia Coppola and Richard Linklater. I gave my nod to Beethoven and Steve Miller, John Ford and Hitchcock.

She said she had never seen *Psycho*, and I told her I would definitely have to walk out on her now.

But as the meal wrapped up she got us back to politics, to basic premises. Her real motive, she told me, was that she felt a responsibility to the poor. That she had been privileged all her life and she wanted to spend the rest of it giving back.

I asked her if she thought the policies of a Genevieve Griffin were the right vehicle for that. She said it was better than what the other side was all about. The other side was truly bad for America, and if we ever went back to those "dark ages," we'd be toast.

The moment was right to ask her about the campaign's strategy. I was hoping the wine would loosen her tongue and she might drop a hint about the Johnson smear. But if she knew anything, it didn't pass her lips.

Nice dinner, though.

Outside, as the valet brought her car around, I got a whiff of her perfume mixing with the ocean air and then we were looking at each other. She almost said something. I almost said something.

Nothing was said.

And not much talk on the way back to my luxury hotel. The atmosphere in the car had changed from cool professionalism to a mild uncertainty. When she dropped me at the corner again she said, "Good luck tomorrow."

"I'll try to stay out of trouble," I said.

I should learn never to say that.

SATURDAY, EARLY EVENING. It was a circus atmosphere outside the church. And I mean that literally. There were jugglers, mimes, a guy on a unicycle, even an animal act—an old man had his terrier doing jumps through a hoop.

The San Francisco Police had a limited presence. The profile of the cops here is that they give wide latitude to "expression," including that which comes without clothing. What a town.

Then there were the news vans and the curious and the street people milling around. I was in charge of one side of the church. I felt like Steve McQueen in *The Magnificent Seven.* "I never rode shotgun on a hearse before." I don't think Steve ever worked security for a house of worship, either.

They'd given me a hand-held two-way that went directly to Kwame. Who was in the church.

I planned not to call him. The less I had to do with him, the better.

Katarina Hogg found me standing on the corner watching all the people go by.

"You look official and intimidating," she said. She was

dressed in a dark-blue suit that form-fitted her in a very pleasing way.

"You look official, too," I said.

"But not intimidating?"

"In the right light, maybe."

She said, "I had a nice time last night. Let's do it again. We can discuss Socrates."

"The unexamined life is not worth living."

After she'd gone I took in a good, long breath of cold air. I slapped my cheeks and decided to do a once-around the church.

It was a good thing I did.

THEY WERE WALKING up the hill with trouble on their minds.

How did I know?

Because one of them held a hand-lettered sign that said, *Ye Shall Have Trouble.*

I met them before they got to the corner. I counted nine of them.

The one with the sign was in front. The ones behind were in a wedge shape, like bowling pins. Which made it easy to stop the whole gang by getting the front guy.

In the dimness I could see he was stringy-limbed and bearded.

"This is fine right here," I said.

"Let us pass," the sign holder said. "We have the right."

Some of the other pins filtered up around him. There were men and women. They had faces like the pioneers in old daguerreotypes—thin, tight mouths, and humorless eyes. I was about to explain the law of Romeo to them when I recognized a face. He recognized me at the same time. The kid from the train.

"It's him!" the kid said.

A man next to the kid came forward, into a tiny pool of light. It was the gray suit guy from the train.

"Hello, Daddy," I said.

"I could have you arrested," he said.

"Careful," I said. "I might be packing peanuts."

"You don't scare me," Daddy said. "I can call a police officer right now."

"And I could give him a real reason to arrest me."

"You are the lost. You are the scum of the earth."

"If you're going to flatter me, you'll have to take me out to dinner, too."

If you can identify the head of a snake, the rest of the slithering backside is easy to handle. All I had to do was keep the old man from moving up the street with his little sign.

I'm sure Kwame would approve, though his own methods would no doubt be a little more ham-fisted.

"Leonard!" Daddy said. From the back shadows came the largest of the tribe. He looked like he'd stepped in from a documentary about the Hell's Angels.

He came up next to Daddy, his eyes alive but in a sort of prison. It was the look of a man who has given up heart and soul to another.

"This is your enforcer?" I said.

"Leonard protects us," Daddy said. "We know there is trouble here."

"Well, Leonard," I said. "Tonight is not your night. I don't want to hurt you. I love butterflies and rainbows, and want to be one with all the animals, but—"

"Do you love sodomites?" Daddy said.

"Maybe he *is* a sodomite," Sonny Boy said. I noticed he was standing behind Leonard. I could see his beady eyes over the big man's shoulder.

I had to be careful. Too much confrontation would bring

unwanted attention to me and this knot of hatred. That might not please Kat or my secret employer back in L.A., Teodor Steadman.

"Get out of the way," Leonard said. He was spoiling for it. I took him as a true convert. Maybe taken in by this church of latter-day dipsticks and delivered from drug addiction or overeating, and giving up his mind to them.

I got ready. I was within finger striking range of Leonard's eyes. You can jab with a fist, but if you extend your finger you get another two or three inches, and you don't need much force to blind a guy for a few seconds. That would be all I needed to finish him with a stun to the neck. That would put him down for a long sleep.

Then one of the men said, "Mud coming."

Daddy and Leonard and Sonny Boy all looked behind them.

I heard a woman's voice, smooth but firm, saying, "Excuse me, please."

No one moved.

"May I get past?" the woman said.

Little by little the bowling pins separated. A nicely dressed black woman, her hair neatly done up on top of her head, made her way to the front. When she got past Daddy, I saw her in the misty glow of the streetlight. She was short and looked to be in her mid sixties. She had a face that was resolute without being angry.

"What goes on here?" She addressed that to me as she came alongside and turned back toward the group. She got a glimpse of the sign Daddy was holding.

"Move along," Leonard ordered her.

She stiffened. "Who are you people?"

"Get going," Daddy said.

"I will not get going," she said. "What do you want trouble for?"

"Let's go," Daddy said and started to charge past us.

Without a second thought I grabbed the sign out of his hands and broke it across my knee.

Leonard reacted the way I knew he would. He came at me like a lumbering bear. I gave him kick to the kneecap and he went down.

"Stop it!" the woman said. "All of you! This is no way to act."

I admired the fire coming out of her.

"Damn your souls to hell," Daddy said.

"How dare you!" the woman said.

"We don't have to listen to this!" Sonny Boy said. Then added, "Do we?"

Leonard, groaning on the ground, said nothing.

"You are outside a church," the woman said. "And you will act with respect."

I loved this woman.

"Fag lover," Daddy said.

"You hush your filthy mouth!" the woman said, drawing her body up to maybe five feet high. To me she looked ten feet tall. I thought she was going to slap Daddy across the face.

But she didn't need to. Daddy was taken aback from her look alone.

"Let's go to the other side of the church," a bowling pin suggested.

"I wouldn't advise that," I said. "This is the friendly side."

"God will rip your entrails from you," Daddy said.

"Oh my Jesus," my companion said. "Don't you dare to speak for God. You march right out of here and repent on your hands and knees!"

Leonard was just getting to his feet but was unsteady on them. He wasn't going to be doing any more enforcing for a while.

"Come on," Daddy said to his rabble. Then to me, "This is not over."

Like ducklings, they fell in behind Daddy as he went marching down the hill. Leonard was the last to follow, limping like he had a wooden leg.

No one offered to help him.

The woman at my side watched them for a moment, then took in a heavy breath.

"Ma'am," I said. "May I escort you to church?"

SABLE WILSON HELD my arm as if I were escorting her to a picnic on a summer's day. She was to meet her grand-daughter inside, she said. The one she'd raised in Oakland. She spoke with love, laced with a tinge of worry. I didn't press her on it. We were at the corner now and turning toward the mass of people in the front of the church. I asked her if she'd like me to take her inside. She said, "No, thank you very much. You are a gentleman," and I decided not to argue the point. I told her how nice it was to meet her and she said, "God bless you."

She started walking then turned to me and added, "He most certainly will."

I watched her as she made her way through the crowd. Something I read came back to me, something written by Viktor Frankl in his book, *Man's Search for Meaning*. There are only two races, he said—the decent and the indecent. Sable Wilson was one of the decent.

I was about to get back to my post when I saw the girl from the campaign office, the dead-eyed envelope stuffer with the tats. She was pacing around on the fringe of the crowd, sucking a cigarette as if it were oxygen. Her pacing took her out into the street then back up on the sidewalk, then back into the street. She was in a tank top again, even though the night was San Francisco cold. She must have had an internal heat pump or maybe a drug-fueled fire. Whatever it was, she was looking for something. Among the street performers and other interested folks, she fit right in.

Two very different women. Sable Wilson at home in her soul and body. And this one, an exposed nerve. I pictured them on a continuum of existence, and wondered where on that line I would fit. Closer to Sable? Or the other?

What direction was I moving?

I decided to go inside. It was almost time for the yakking to begin. I wanted to hear it, even though Kwame told me I wasn't supposed to come in. Maybe that was the main reason I did.

Before entering I made one more round of the exterior. I didn't see Leonard or the protesters. But I did see the lights of the Golden Gate Bridge. A lovely invitation to get out of town.

I PICKED A spot in one of the back corners of the church and looked around. What was supposed to be a sacred space now had the feel of a horse auction. The buyers were standing and babbling to each other, while the saints in the stained-glass windows looked down with bemused detachment. One of the icons was holding out his hand as if to perform a miracle. From his simple habit, I thought it might be Saint Francis of Assisi. He was a man who left everything behind to go and serve the poor and love animals and challenge the pope. I guess if you're going to do anything, you might as well go all the way.

At other spots in the church stood Kwame's dogs. They looked like boys playing soldier. I didn't spot Kwame himself. Maybe he was in a room taking his nightly dose of bile.

A pool news camera was set up behind the back pews. The tripod was next to the font of holy water. The sacred and the profane. Perfect.

On the other side of the church, I saw Sable sitting in a dignified silence. Next to her was the young woman I figured was her granddaughter. She was fidgeting with something in her lap. Sable put her hand on her in a calming gesture. The young woman sat back like a petulant child being told what to do.

Finally, Jay J. Parsons made his way down the center aisle, pausing every now and then to glad-hand. By this time the place was stuffed. The air was stuffier. Stained-glass windows are not known for their ventilation.

Up on the stage sat Father Dwayne Weaver, decked out in green-and-gold priestly robes. Kat Hogg sat next to him.

Jay J made his way up the steps to the stage. He talked a little to Kat, then to Weaver. Then he laughed. Then he went to the podium and tapped the microphone. "Testing, testing," he said. Satisfied, he asked people to find a seat.

The place gradually came to order.

"How's everybody doin' tonight?" Jay J said.

The crowd whooped it up.

"Yeah! That's what I'm talkin' about! Are we ready to get it on?"

The people responded with more whoops. Yes. They were ready to get it on.

"Are you ready to kick Samuel Johnson's butt?"

Yes, they were ready to kick Samuel Johnson's butt.

"And reelect Genevieve Griffin?"

Oh, yes.

"Are you ready to keep America safe from the fanatics?"

They screamed like fanatics.

"All right then! Put your hands together and welcome the man himself, Dr. Rodney Shipp!"

The place went nuts. Rodney Shipp walked out onto the stage and gave Jay J. Parsons a hug. Then he went to the foot of the stage and smiled. He put his hands out like he was blessing the people.

I belched.

After about a minute the place quieted down and Shipp began.

"Tonight I'm honored to address you folks, the good folks of the golden city, where hope remains vibrant and alive and full of love in your hearts."

Applause and whoops.

"A little over twenty years ago, the Reverend Jesse Jackson stood up at the Democratic National Convention right here in San Francisco and talked about freedom. It was a speech that made history, a black man at the podium, talking about the great hope that we still fight for today. Just last week, though, I had the distinct displeasure to listen to another black man talk about taking us back to the past. His name is Samuel Johnson."

Boos and jeers. It sure didn't take much to rile this audience.

"No, no, this is not about popularity. This is about ideas and the promise of America. The promise of America says we will guarantee quality education for all children and not spend more money on metal detectors than computers in the classroom."

Cheers.

"The promise of America does not seek to regulate your behavior in the bedroom, but it does guarantee your right to have food in the kitchen. The promise of America is that we stand for human rights, whether it's fighting against slavery in the Sudan and for immigration at home, a chance for all to succeed. Are you with me?"

They were with him.

"Will you stand with your great senator, Genevieve Griffin?"

They would.

"Will you tell Samuel Johnson to keep his nose in his books and not bother us with his dangerous ideas?"

Oh yes, definitely.

He went on. And on. His talk was peppered with the cadence of the Pentecostal preacher and the Old West snake-oil salesman. He got louder. The church got stuffier.

And Father Weaver looked like he was sitting on thumbtacks.

"Then go on to tell all your friends and neighbors not to stay home on voting day. This is too great a danger facing us. We are never going back. And if they try, there will be no peace. No peace from us. No rest. Justice is what we expect, and justice is what we will get!"

The place rocked.

Somebody started singing, and soon the whole place was like a revival meeting.

That's what they want, after all, the movers, shakers, and president makers. Not deliberation but enthusiasm. Not thought but shouts.

And Dr. Rodney Shipp ate it up like an ice cream sundae.

Jay J. Parsons got the crowd to quiet down long enough for him to introduce Father Weaver. This being his church, he got the last word. But there was clearly alpha-dogging between him and Shipp.

When he got up, the crowd gave him a respectful silence. He started pacing.

"Brothers and sisters, tonight I speak up on behalf of God's people, the weak and the halt, the poor and the prisoners! In this world there is room for everyone. And the good earth is rich and can provide for everyone. The way of life can be free and beautiful, but we have lost the way."

He spoke as if the words were a fire in his belly. I had to admit he was good.

"Greed has poisoned people's souls, has barricaded the world with hate, has goose-stepped us into misery and bloodshed. We have developed speed, but we have shut ourselves in. Machinery that gives abundance has left us in want. Our knowledge has made us cynical. Our cleverness, hard and unkind. We think too much and feel too little. More than machinery we need humanity. More than cleverness we need kindness and gentleness. Without these qualities, life will be violent and all will be lost."

Boy, those were good words. But they sounded familiar to me. Like they were from an old movie, or newsreel ... wait ... *The Great Dictator*. One of my dad's favorite movies. Weaver was doing a Charlie Chaplin speech!

"To those who can hear me, I say: do not despair. You, the people, have the power to make this life free and beautiful, to make this life one of justice and peace. But only if you listen to the voice of God crying in your souls. Don't listen to men. Don't even listen to me! Listen to your hearts."

There were some *amens* then, and a few cheers. But up on stage Dr. Rodney Shipp was muttering to one of the men on his left.

"Don't be told what to do anymore," Weaver said. "Listen to your own heart and walk with God to a new dawn and a new day. Come with me on this journey. We are in this together! We are—"

He didn't get a chance to finish.

IT WAS A smoke bomb. White, acrid clouds billowing all over the front of the church.

Screams and panic and bumping bodies. People must have thought there were guns in the house of the Lord. They crushed toward the aisles and exits.

Haze blanketed the altar and Father Weaver. In the middle of it all, I saw Kwame's men moving into some sort of action focused on the front of the church. Since I was part of the security squad for the night, I followed.

I pushed my way through the panic, banked right, got to an

open door leading to the back. One of Kwame's men was in front of it, arms folded. He just stared at me.

"Really?" I said.

"Only our folks."

"I *am* your folks."

He shoved me in the chest.

I stumbled back a couple of steps, hit something. Heard a woman cry out. Turning, I saw a heavy-set woman on the floor, legs splayed. Good thing she was wearing pants.

I helped her to her feet and apologized.

She gave me an unforgiving look as her mouth uttered a word that should not be heard inside a house of God, and very few places outside.

I turned back to the dog at the door. He was smiling.

He shook his head in warning.

I smiled and nodded, put my foot behind his as I pushed his face. He fell backward and down some steps. His head made a resonant thump. I stepped over him and went down a couple more steps into a corridor with a series of doors. Looked like classrooms.

I looked through door number one, nothing, then door number two.

Pay dirt.

It was a nursery. There were four of the Dogs and Kwame. They had her in a chair, a little chair for a little girl. One of the Dogs was holding her arms behind her, hard.

Tattoo Girl yelped in pain then cursed like the curator of Urban Dictionary.

"Hold it," I said.

Kwame turned on me. "Get out!"

"Let her go," I said.

"Get him out!"

One of the Dogs came toward me. "Hold on," I said. "This is police matter now."

"Police? They ain't never gonna know."

"They will if I tell them," I said.

"You ain't gonna tell them."

The Dog at my side repeated, "You ain't gonna tell them."

"Shut up!" Kwame said. "Just take him out and make sure he don't come back."

The guy reached for the baton in his belt. I kicked the bottom of his chin with my heel. He crashed backwards over a craft table. Glue and crayons and construction paper scattered.

Everyone in the room seemed to take a collective breath. I needed to take advantage of the moment.

I gave Kwame my signature move from cage days. Gripping his left arm like a joystick I got him down to one knee and wrapped my right leg around his neck. I held him there like a giant nutcracker with a pistachio at the ready.

"Nobody move or Kwame becomes physically challenged."

Nobody moved.

"Let the girl go," I said.

The Dog holding her arms did not let go.

I flexed my leg and Kwame grunted and sucked for air.

"Let her go," I said.

A pause. A thought. A look. And then the guard dog let her go.

"Get out of here," I told her.

She didn't have to be asked twice. She ran out the door.

Which made for a rather embarrassing tableau. I was holding Kwame, head of security, in the crook of my leg. Four other military-dressed hard guys were frozen in positions of what-do-I-do-now?

And into the room walked Dr. Rodney Shipp with two bodyguards.

"What goes on here?" he said.

"A little security problem," I said.

"Who are you? Let that man go."

"Tell him to cool off and I will."

Shipp looked down at Kwame and back at me. "You better be sure what you're doing."

I unwrapped my leg from around Kwame's head and let him up. He took a swing at me. I ducked it, grabbed his wrist, and put him down on his knees again. And held him there.

"No more of that," Shipp said.

Kat and Jay J. Parsons appeared at the door. "You have the person," Parsons said. "A woman. Where is she?"

"Good question," Shipp said.

Dwayne Weaver breezed in. Now the room was starting to resemble a fraternity prank.

I said, "Your boys were about to do something really stupid that would've brought you a lot of bad publicity. Here in the church. Assaulting a suspect."

"You're a dead man," Kwame said.

I twisted his arm.

He growled through his teeth.

"Stop it," Shipp said. "Let him up. Please."

Since he said please, I let Kwame up.

And up was what Kwame got, fast, like he was going to try me then and there. But he looked at Shipp and then just pointed at me.

"Who are you?" Shipp asked.

Parsons said, "He's somebody we hired." Then to me, "You're fired. You don't work for us anymore."

Kat said, "Jay J, don't do this—"

"No. That's it." He looked at me like a wimp showing off because the big boys were there. "Get out and get gone."

"Let him stay," Kwame said. "Let him stay with me."

"All right," Shipp said. "Let it go." To me he said, "Sir, you are excused."

"It's been lovely being with you all," I said.

"You better leave the city," Kwame said.

"I haven't picked up my sourdough yet," I said.

THE CORRIDOR SMELLED like the Fourth of July. I was almost out the rear exit when Kat caught up with me.

"Where will you go?" she asked.

"Outside."

"I want to talk."

"I don't like who you run with."

She held my arm. "Give me a chance."

"You have a car?"

"Across the street."

There was all sorts of chaos outside, people milling around, oncoming sirens in the distance. Kat's Subaru was down the block.

"Drive somewhere," I said. "Somewhere away from here. Then find a place to pull over."

She drove several blocks, fighting traffic on the way. The center of activity was now the church, and why not? It had everything—politics, a bomb, TV. It was a natural for the news.

Kat found a spot to pull over on a tiny street in what I think was Russian Hill.

"Okay, what's going on?" she said.

"What do you know about Kwame's men and the kind of people they are?"

"Everybody pretty much knows. Shipp keeps them in line."

"Are you that naïve?"

"I'm not! I know there are costs."

"That's a great way to look at human lives."

"Now who's naïve?" she said.

She had a point. "There's a girl who works at the campaign office. A lot of tattoos. Heavy black makeup. You know the one?"

"Yes."

"They had her, Kwame's crew. They thought she was the one who delivered the smoke bomb. Does she seem like that kind of person to you?"

"I don't know her."

"Who would have hired her?"

"Jay J. Or maybe Monique."

"Who's Monique?"

"She works for Genevieve. She has her hands in a lot of things."

"Do you have a way of finding out who this girl is?"

"Sure. We have all the contact information."

"Access it."

"Why?"

"We have to find her. Before Kwame does."

I should have let it go then. This wasn't my business. It wasn't what I was sent up here for. But then again, this tattooed girl had something going on I needed to know about. I could find out more from her than from Kat, at least right now. I'd use Kat to find her and then put the Kat out the door.

Kat pulled out a tablet and started fingering around. Presently she said, "Here it is. Her name is Leeza. Leeza Edgar. She lives on Van Ness."

"Take me there."

WE DROVE TO the address. It was a dumpy building. Or an arty building if you were in a good mood. Kat pulled in front of a driveway across from the building.

"What do you expect to do?" she asked.

"Wait for her, then talk. Find out why she did it."

"You think she'll tell us?"

"I think she'll give me some credit for getting her out of there."

"This is nuts," Kat said. "Why would she do such a thing?"

"If she did."

"What do you mean?"

"Maybe she's what they used to call a fall guy. We don't know anything except there was a smoke bomb and Kwame thought she did it. For all we know *he* did it. There's some sort of rivalry between Shipp and Weaver."

"How do you know that?"

"Am I wrong?"

She shook her head.

"Wait here." I got out and crossed the street. Edgar was on the directory. I buzzed and got nothing.

I went back and got in Kat's car.

"So we wait," I said. "Unless you want to go. I can hoof back to my hotel."

"No way," she said. "We're in this together now. I'm out on a limb with you."

"How do you like it?"

She put her hand on the back of my neck and pulled me into a kiss.

It was her play. I let her. And I kissed her back.

She knew how to kiss.

Then just as quickly it was over and she put both her hands on the steering wheel and looked forward.

"Unbelievable," she said.

"I believed it," I said.

She shook her head. "I'm talking about me. I don't do that."

"It's okay."

"Can we just forget that I did that?"

"That would take some brain surgery," I said.

"Un-freaking-believable."

"It's all right," I said. I put my left on her right, which was tight around the wheel.

"Mike?"

"Hmm?"

"Can I ask you a personal question?"

"After that kiss? Ask away."

"What happened to your hand?"

She was looking at my left and the jagged white scar around the base of the little finger.

"Unfortunate accident," I said.

"Did you work in a sawmill or something?" she said lightly, but wanting to know the truth.

"It was just one of those things."

"That's random," she said.

"It was severed, but a nice doctor sewed it back on."

She just stared at me.

"I've grown rather attached to it," I said.

She tried not to smile but finally couldn't help it.

"Go ahead," I said. "Sometimes you have to laugh or you'll cry."

She said, "I want to know about you. But I'm ..."

"Go ahead," I said.

She didn't say anything.

"Fear nothing," I said. "That's rule number one."

"You are so random," she said.

"There's that word again. So you really believe it?"

"That you're random?"

"That there's no order in the universe."

Shaking her head, she smiled and said, "Where do you get all this?"

That's when I saw Leeza Edgar running up to the door of her building.

I BOLTED ACROSS the street and got her before she cracked the door.

She jumped back like I was the guy from *Friday the 13th*.

"I don't think you're safe here," I said.

"What the h—"

"No time to talk. Come with me."

I put my hand out. She slapped it. "Get away from me."

"I'm on your side," I said.

She began a tirade then, peppered with words with a hard K sound. She was a symphony of K. It was so constant and crazy, it hit my brain like *woodpecker woodpecker peck peck woodpecker*.

"Ease up," I said. "There's bad people who want you. Did you forget that?"

Woodpecker woodpecker!

"Your boss, one of your bosses, Kat Hogg, is in a car over there. Come with us."

Leeza looked across the street. Then she turned and ran.

I said something that sounded like *woodpecker* myself and gave chase.

She was fast, this one. A little tattooed gazelle. But I had longer legs.

I caught her at the corner and put a vise grip on her arm.

Peck peck woodpecker!

A couple of white guys from retro-grunge central came toward us. I could smell the ganj from twenty feet away.

"Let go of my arm!" Leeza said.

"What up?" one of the retros said. He was tall and white and stringy, hair packed into a Rasta knit cap.

"Move on," I said.

"You oughta let her go, man." He had the red eyes and thick speech of the freshly baked. His partner took a suck on a pipe and held the smoke in.

"Not your business," I said.

"Lemme go!" Leeza shouted.

"Let her go, man."

"I'm her probation officer," I said. "She's been selling weed to teenagers."

Leeza un-nested more *woodpeckers*.

Rasta Cap said, "You're no probation guy."

Kat's car came tearing up the street. She stopped and called at me to get in.

"Kidnapping!" Leeza screamed.

"Hey!" Rasta Cap said. He stepped up to me like he was going to do something about it. Holding Leeza with my left hand, I pulled the knit cap over the guy's face, then took his legs out from under him with a side sweep.

"You're under arrest," I said. "Stay here until I get back."

I opened the back of Kat's car and pushed Leeza in.

AS KAT DROVE, Leeza became all flailing arms and legs and cursing.

I put my hand under her chin and squeezed her mouth. Her lips protruded like a beak.

"Cut it out," I said. "I don't want to hear another F word out of you. You're giving me an effing headache."

She tried to say something through her mashed lips. It sounded like *fuff oo*.

I squeezed harder. "Do you like this?"

She didn't respond. I rotated her head side to side. "No," I said. "You don't like this. And if you go back to being out of control I'm going to do this to you again. Are we clear?"

I nodded her head.

"Don't test me," I said. I took my hand away. She opened her mouth and almost said something. Then stopped.

"Where you taking me?" she said.

"We just want to talk," Kat said.

"I ain't sayin' nothin'."

"Nobody's asked you anything," I said.

"I ain't gonna say nothin' no matter what anybody asks me."

"You can talk to us or you can talk to the guys back at the church," I said. "We can drop her off at the church, can't we, Kat?"

"We can do that," Kat said.

Kat was cresting a hill. The view of the bay and lights and a low-hanging fog suggested a good night for lovers or serial killers.

"Just let me go," Leeza said. "It doesn't matter."

"What doesn't matter?" I said.

"Anything." She looked at her hands. There were tiny marks on the backs.

"Why'd you do it?" I said.

Leeza said nothing.

"The smoke bomb," I said.

No answer.

"You have something against Weaver? The church? The Democratic party?"

Zip.

"To get attention?" I said.

Her head snapped up.

"That's it, isn't it?" I said. "You did it to make a name."

She went back to *woodpecker* mode. I put my hand up and she stopped talking.

"Leeza," Kat said. "How about something to eat?"

KAT TOOK US to a small Italian place by the Wharf.

Leeza ate like a prisoner from Devil's Island. When she finally slowed down, she said she wanted to go outside and have a cigarette. I told Kat to order up some dessert. As long as the Democratic Party was paying, I was okay with it. For once they'd be redistributing their own money.

"You should give that up," I said to Leeza as she fired up an unfiltered Camel.

"Shut up," she said.

"Try vaping."

"Shut *up*."

We were by the lamppost just outside the restaurant. The bustle of normal night life was happening around us. The fog had creeped in, moistening everything.

"How old are you?" I said.

"Shut up," she said.

"I'm sensing you're not into conversation."

She blew a stream of smoke into the night air. "How come you don't talk like a normal person?"

"How about you tell me why you did the smoke bomb. What did you expect?"

"Nothin'."

"Who are you mad at?"

"Nobody."

"Then why do it?"

"Are you sleeping with her?" she said.

"Why should I tell you?" I said.

"So you are."

"That's not your business, is it?"

"I'm not your business," she said.

"Right now I wish you weren't," I said. "But you're in trouble."

"I'm so not. Nobody cares if I live or die."

"Shut up," I said.

She fought a smile by plugging her mouth with the cigarette. And I stood there wondering what the best and fastest way to get out of San Francisco would be. I'd do my job, what there was of it, and go back and collect my money. Politics was getting tiresome.

It was about to get a lot more than that.

You can sense when a car has bad intentions. This was a black Cadillac sedan, coming up slowly as if to drop someone off. But when the window started down I didn't think it was to ask for directions. A hand came out with metal in it. I grabbed Leeza and wrapped myself around her. Three pops split the air. One shot got me in the back. Down I went, still holding Leeza. I hit my head on something hard.

The last thing I heard before I passed out sounded like *woodpecker* ...

IN THE GREEK myth, Hades was the brother of Zeus and Poseidon. But he didn't get to be king of Olympus, or the ruler of the sea.

He got stuck with the underworld, which teed him off no end. One day he was sitting around when he caught sight of a maiden named Persephone, and what a sight she was. A finer looking Greek personification of womanhood there was not. Hades decided he'd have her, so one fine spring morning as she was gathering flowers, Hades popped out of a crack in the earth, grabbed her, and took to the underworld and, as they used to say, had his way with her.

Persephone's mother, Demeter, was beside herself, and looked all over, but couldn't find her daughter. So being in charge of the fertility of the Earth, she didn't let anything grow. Naturally, that made people hungry, and they shouted about that to Zeus, who didn't like noise. So he went to Hades and said, "Dude, you bring her back right now."

Hades was always competing with his big brother. So before releasing Persephone, he tricked her into tasting an underworld pomegranate. A few seeds, that's all. And because she had tasted of the underworld, she was now forced to spend the winter months down in the underworld with Hades.

Hades changed his name to Pluto, but everybody knew

who he was. But then people started to call the underworld Hades, the realm of the dead.

Which is where I was at the moment.

Wandering around in some dreamscape, until I found myself standing in front of a pomegranate tree. Hot I was, and hungry.

Someone said, "Don't eat that."

I turned and saw a beautiful woman.

"Persephone?"

She nodded.

"You don't want to stay here," she said.

"I'm hungry."

"Somebody needs you. Go back."

She disappeared then, and I felt myself swimming through a sea of pea soup, fighting for air, wanting to sink back in and sleep, sleep in the warm soup and never come out. But somebody was telling me to wake up. My head poked through the muck and I tried to open my eyes. They fought me on this.

"Up, up, come on now." The voice was a woman's. Not a friendly woman, either.

My eyelids were flour bags. Just let me sleep.

"Up now. Come on, Mr. Romeo."

Bright light seeped in through my eye slits. I managed to turn my head. A nurse stood there. I assume it was a nurse.

My right shoulder hurt. I tried to say something but my tongue was thick and lazy.

Then I remembered.

Shots.

Leeza.

I made my mouth ask what day it was.

"Sunday," the nurse said.

My lids clamped down. I felt a hand on my good shoulder. "No sleeping," the nurse said. "Up, up, up!"

"Leeza," I said.

"What's that, Mr. Romeo?"

"Leeeeeza."

"Is that a name?"

"Kat."

"Family?"

"Get me out."

"Now you just wake up and we'll get you all taken care of."

An hour later, the nurse wheeled me into a room with a couple other beds. Both beds had men in them. The man in the middle had tubes in his nose and was asleep. He had white hair and a dapper white mustache and two days' worth of beard.

On the other side of him was a whale of a man lying on top of his sheets. Some white blubber seeped through his inadequate hospital gown. He had no hair on his head, but did on his big arms which were folded across his chest. He scowled at me like I was a slow waiter at Denny's.

The nurse waited until I was in the bed, then showed me how to adjust it with the handset. She poured me some water from a plastic jug, and put a baggie with my wallet and phone in the drawer of the bed table.

"A little privacy," I said.

She drew the pale curtain so Dapper Dan and Whale Man couldn't see me.

I called Ira.

"It's about time," Ira said.

"There's been a setback," I said.

"Oh boy."

"I got shot."

"What?"

"It was a mistake. At least I think it was. I think they were after a girl I was with."

"You were with a girl?"

"I'll explain later. But I'm temporarily indisposed."

"Where are you?"

"Hospital."

"How bad are you?"

"I don't know yet."

"I'll come up there."

"No need. I'll be out of here soon enough and then I'm going hunting."

"Hunting?"

"You can do something for me," I said.

"What do you mean by hunting?" Ira said.

"I need an address. Sable Wilson is the name. Somewhere in Oakland."

"Sable Wilson?"

"That's it."

"You want to hang on?" Ira said.

"I've got nothing better to do," I said.

Ira grumbled. He has a way of doing that sometimes. It means he loves me.

About ninety seconds later he said, "I found a Sable Wilson on 85th Street. She's owned her home since 1975. A widow."

"Give me the address."

He did. I left-thumbed it into my phone.

Then he said, "Now, back to the hunting thing. I don't want you to hunt anyone. Have the police talked to you yet?"

"Not yet."

"Keep everything confidential," Ira said.

"Of course."

"Call me again soon."

"After I go hunting."

"Mike!"

"Thanks for your help."

"Don't hang—"

I hung up.

And thought I could hear Ira's grumble all the way up here.

· · ·

A DOCTOR CAME in a few minutes later. He was black and looked like he was just about to have his twenty-first birthday. He wore an unbuttoned white smock over hospital blues and cocked his head slightly to the right when he talked. It was like he was looking for something else wrong with me.

"How we feeling?" he said.

"I don't know about you," I said, "but I'd rather be in Philadelphia."

He smiled. "I hear you. I'm Dr. Parker. I pulled the bullet out of you last night."

"Do I get to keep it?" I said.

"I'm afraid it's evidence," Dr. Parker said. "The bullet hit you just to the left of your right scapula, the wing bone, so no damage there. It may have hit a rib and it might have turned in a spinal direction, but you've got some mighty tough musculature, my friend. The bullet stuck in your traps and didn't move far at all."

"Sort of like a flaming arrow in a Roman shield?"

"Excuse me?"

"The Romans used leather on their shields and wet them to put out flaming arrows."

"I did not know that."

"What kind of medical schools have they got these days?"

He cocked his head to the other side, so I decided to quit talking. He told me a cop would be in to see me soon.

My day was looking better and better.

FIVE MINUTES LATER Kat came in. "Thank God you're all right." She slid a chair to my bed.

"I look all right to you?" I said.

"Have the police talked to you yet?"

"No."

"I gave them a statement. Thank God." She put her right hand on my left.

"How's Leeza?" I said.

"She took off."

"When?"

"Right after it happened," Kat said. "I came outside to see where you were and there was a crowd around and you were on the ground, blood all over your back."

"The cops have any leads?"

She said, "I heard one man tell them he got a plate, and they wore masks."

"That won't help."

"Why not?"

"The plates'll be counterfeit," I said.

She touched my arm. "Mike, I thought you were dead."

"Who would want to kill a nice guy like me?" I said. "Maybe they were after Leeza."

"It's so bizarre."

"Is it?" I said.

Kat took her hand away, put it in her lap. "Why would you say that?"

"You've got those Dogs on the payroll."

"Not *our* payroll," she said.

"You're all part of the same bowl of nuts," I said.

"Now wait a minute, Mike, that's not fair."

"What's unfair about it?"

"This isn't the time," Kat said.

"Soon as I can, I'm heading back to L.A.," I said.

"But why?"

"Nothing to keep me here."

"Nothing?" she said.

I said, "Los Angeles and San Francisco don't mix."

"I don't think I want you to go," she said.

"I don't mix, either," I said. "I'm not good at it. Things like this happen to me all the time. I'm unsafe."

"Mike—"

"I'm not good at hospital scenes, either," I said. "Do me a favor and just go."

She studied my eyes.

"Without a big thing," I said.

"Do you really want me to?"

"Yeah."

She stood up then. Her expression was a mix of anger and hurt. But not hate.

I could live with that.

She turned and left the room.

I had ten minutes of regret. Then a cop came in.

"YOUR NAME IS Mike Romeo?" he said. He was plain clothes, a shield on his belt.

I didn't feel like talking. I felt like biting off my tubes. But as I had been shot by a man with a gun, I guess I owed him some time. His name was Swaggert.

"Yes," I said.

"Says *Mike* on your license, not *Michael*."

"Right."

"Guess your folks like shorthand."

"Do you have any real questions?"

"Easy there. Just making conversation. You're not in any hurry, are you?"

"I am, as a matter of fact."

"Go ahead and tell me what happened."

"Somebody popped me on the streets of San Francisco."

"What do you remember about it?"

"Just the car. A black Cadillac. I didn't have time to see the faces. Somebody said they had masks on."

"That's right."

"And somebody got a plate?"

"That's right, too. Only it was a fake plate."

"Professionals," I said.

"There was a young woman involved."

"Yeah. Leeza Edgar, that's Leeza with a Z."

"What is your relationship with this woman?"

"None. I got her out of some trouble and was having dinner with her. She wanted a smoke so we went outside, and that's when the car came by. I acted on instinct, covered her up."

"How did you know there were going to be shots?"

"Just a feeling."

"That's a pretty good feeling. What is it you do, Mr. Romeo?"

"Private security."

"Uh-huh. So you thought shots were coming, you protected the woman?"

"That's how it worked out."

"Where is she now?"

"I don't know."

"Was anybody else with you?"

"Not outside."

"Inside?"

"Another dinner guest."

"Name?"

"Let's leave her out of it, okay?"

"Let's not."

"She's not relevant to the investigation."

"How about you let me decide what's relevant?"

"How about I stop answering questions now?"

"You're making things difficult, Mr. Romeo."

"I'm just that kind of guy. What you really should be asking is how a car fires shots and then gets away."

"I'm sure we're asking that question. When you got hit, what happened next?"

"I fell forward and hit my head. Conked out. When I came to, Leeza was gone. She was under me last I remembered."

"You say you just met this woman?"

"Pretty much."

"So you don't know any reason why anybody would take a shot at her?"

"None."

"Could have been a random drive by."

"Could have, but I wouldn't bet on it."

"Maybe they were shooting at you."

"I thought about that. But I'm new in town. Not a very friendly town, I have to say."

"You live in L.A.?"

"Currently."

"How long you been down there?"

"How is that relevant?"

"Don't start that again."

"I'm not a Dodger fan or a Giant hater, if that's what you mean."

Finally he smiled. "Who do you like?"

"Red Sox," I said. "My dad loved Yastrzemski."

"I'm from across the bay. A's fan. The Bash Brothers."

"McGuire and Canseco."

"Before the juice," he said. "Anyway, I'm going to ask that you not leave the city in the next few days, okay?"

"Material witness?"

"You got it."

"I'm not exactly going anywhere," I said.

"Where can I reach you?"

"I'm staying at The Serene."

"Whoa," he said.

"I know," I said.

"Not exactly a place for fine gentlemen."

"I fit right in," I said.

He nodded, wished me well, left the room.

I LOOKED AT the ceiling and lost myself in the holes for a while.

I started to think about curses. There's karma, of course, and there's just desserts. There's Greek tragedy and Ecclesiastes. You don't always get what you pay for, but maybe you always pay for your sins.

What was I doing here, shot up?

Paying for it. Paying for the man I'd killed in New Haven.

My father would have been horrified.

My mother would have wept.

But I did what I did, in the grip of the black fog that changed everything for me forever. That Tuesday ...

I WAS EATING a Pop-Tart by a window in the Sterling library and getting into a book. I remember all this clearly. The Pop-Tart was brown sugar cinnamon. The book was a collection of ancient essays, and the one I was in at the moment was Cicero's *Treatise on Friendship and Old Age.* The dead Roman was having a conversation with me. I was lonely at Yale, didn't connect with many people ever, but I was connecting with Cicero and hoping I could find someday, with someone, what Cicero described as *complete accord on all subjects human and divine, joined with mutual goodwill and affection.*

At one point, I looked out the window at the changing leaves, gold and red and orange, with the sun on them, and for that moment it felt like I could start my life *afresh,* as I used to put it. I was always looking for the right time to have a fresh start. Put away all the muck of the past and start forward with new feet, new feeling.

The leaves were a collage of hope, and then I saw the people running.

Students, old and young, running like someone was chasing them.

Next thing I knew a door flies open and a campus security guard, his face flushed and scared, screamed at everybody to get down on the floor.

I thought it was a joke, one of the frat boys in costume, but then he said it again and I knew he meant it.

"There's a shooter! Get down!" He fumbled for some keys and was trying to lock the doors from the inside.

People started yelling and asking what was going on and the guard kept yelling and fumbling. Some people hit the ground, but I didn't. I wanted to keep watching outside, I wanted to know for certain what was going on. A little worm of dread was moving around in my stomach, something instinctive. I knew death was out there somewhere. I was outside myself watching this, wondering what would happen if everybody in the library died. Including me.

Yes, a meditation on death by the fat genius who didn't have any friends. Not exactly the makings of a hit TV show.

We stayed on lockdown for forty minutes or so, the guard using his crackling walkie-talkie to keep up to speed. Finally the guard stood up and said it was all clear, but that we were to proceed up York Street to the law school, and *not* to go toward Connecticut Hall.

Where the philosophy department was.

Where my mom was meeting with my dad, and where I was going to meet up with them for lunch.

The world turned dark blue, underwater colors, deep sea. I was trying to get to the surface but there was something pulling me down. I left my backpack and ran, bumping people, saying *sorry, sorry* but not stopping. But the guard put his hands on me and said, "Slowly. To the law school."

"Sure," I lied, and walked outside the doors and turned started running the wrong way.

It was almost noon and the sun was shining, but it was the reflection of knife blades on me, every part of my skin cut. Bleeding inside I ran.

Right into the police cordon at Elm Street.

A female cop saw me and shook her head and waved at me to go back.

I didn't listen.

"My mom and dad are in Connecticut Hall!" I said.

"You can't come in here," she said. "It's a crime scene."

"What happened?"

"You'll have to go to the law school now. Someone will fill you in."

"Please tell me!"

"I can't tell you anything now." She tried to turn me around but I slapped her hand away and ran past her.

It wasn't a close race. A male cop tackled me after about a fifty-yard dash. My face hit the pavement and I was crying and screaming *pleeeeaaassse ...*

The cop put cuffs on me, behind my back, and picked me up by the shirt collar. He walked me over to an ambulance and made me sit on the ground. He spoke to a paramedic about doing something about me. Watch me till he came back.

The paramedic was around thirty, spoke with an Indian accent. "You know somebody who was shot?" he said.

"How many?" I managed to say.

"We don't know yet."

"There was a shooter?"

"He's dead. Shot himself."

"Was he inside the building? Connecticut?"

"Inside and outside," the paramedic said.

"God, my mom and dad!"

"They were there?"

"Yes!"

"All right, all right, there are lots of people who've come out of there. Lots."

"I've gotta find out!" I started to get to my feet but the paramedic gently pushed me down.

"Just hang with me," he said.

There were sirens and more ambulances and, in the distance, a scream. This one not of fear but of abject horror.

I rolled onto my side and cried into the street. I felt the hand of the paramedic on my back.

WHEN THE COP came back he had Brenda Phelps with him. She was a gray-haired office administrator. I'd known her my whole life, and she was barking at the cop to get those cuffs off me, and who did he think he was doing that to me?

In a moment I was free and before I could ask where my parents were, Brenda pulled me into her ample frame with strong arms and said, "Oh dear boy, dear boy ..."

And that's when I knew.

My wailing was muted and lost in her chest.

THE FINAL COUNT was eighteen, including the shooter who offed himself when the cops started closing in.

Office workers, interns, students and two professors—Dr. Rexford Chamberlain and Dr. Rosemary Brayshaw Chamberlain.

My dad and mom.

The shooter was a medical student named Benjamin Weeden Blackpoole.

It would be another two years before I killed a man named Thurber McDaniels ...

I WOKE UP.

Sweating. Thinking about karma. About payback.

About me getting what I deserved.

About trying to do something with my life to restore a balance.

There wasn't a balance here in San Francisco.

The guy in the bed next to me was watching TV. A woman in a tight dress was standing sideways as the big weather map moved around.

When was I going to get out of here?

The weather woman gave a fetching smile and the camera went back to the toothy anchors, a man and a woman. Then the woman took over, and behind her was the headshot of another woman. I recognized her face but couldn't remember the name.

Then they switched to a shot of the same woman sitting in front of microphones in what looked like a law office. Next to her was a young black woman who also looked familiar. Who I also could not place.

There was some yakkety yakkety.

Then they went to a shot of Samuel Johnson coming out of his house, toward his car. A camera and reporter rushed up, ambush-style. Johnson waved them off, got into his car. As he backed out of his driveway the camera followed, but Johnson made no statement.

There is no way to look innocent when the news guys do that to you.

I buzzed for the nurse. When she got there I told her I was ready to go. She told me a doctor would be in to see me. I told her to get him in before I took out the IV and walked out. A doctor, an Indian-American, came in to calm me down. We reasoned together. I was a guy with no money and no insurance, and here's your bed. He kept telling me about the physical therapy I'd have to find, and I told him thank you, I will, and now let's clean up this mess.

He nodded and mumbled something.

I told him I needed a shirt and he said he'd arrange for one from their benevolence room. He said I looked like a big guy and the shirt might be tight. I told him not to worry, I wasn't going to go pose on the beach.

An hour later I was wearing a lime-green golf shirt with a logo on the left breast, a cartoon of a blue gel tab with a smiling face. Under the gel tab in yellow script it said *Blaxx Pharmaceuticals.*

They fitted me with a sling and gave me some papers telling me how to take care of a wound. With my left hand I signed the CYA paper, and then they took me down to the entrance.

KAT WAS WAITING for me. The nurse stopped my wheelchair in front of her.

"You don't know how to take no for an answer, do you?" I said.

"You need me," she said. "Besides, you owe me a drink."

"For what?"

"The campaign is going to pay for your hospital stay."

The nurse said, "That's good news, isn't it?"

I got out of the chair. "Thanks for the ride," I said.

"Good luck, Mr. Romeo," the nurse said.

Outside the front doors I said, "You fired me. Why pay?"

Kat said, "You saved one of our volunteers."

"Even though she threw a smoke bomb in church?" I said.

"Nobody's perfect." She looked me over. "Does it hurt?"

"Only when somebody asks me if it hurts," I said.

"Let's go," she said.

"Where?"

"My place. So you can rest."

"No," I said. "Take me to Parsons."

"You can't walk around with your wound."

"They didn't shoot my legs. Take me to Parsons."

JAY J. PARSONS stood up like there was a mouse under his desk.

"What's he—"

"Relax, Jay J," Kat said. "He just wants to talk to you."

"I fired his butt."

"You don't know the whole story," Kat said.

Parsons looked at me warily. "You look terrible. What happened?"

"Bowling," I said.

"What—"

Kat said, "He got shot. He saved Leeza Edgar's life."

Parsons sat back down. "I don't believe this. Where is she?"

"We don't know," Kat said.

"But maybe you do," I said.

"Me?"

I nodded.

"How should I know?"

"Because you're sleeping with her," I said.

A pinkness like the inside of a rare steak came to his face. It started at the cheek level and moved up to his forehead where it stopped on the beaches of his bald pate.

"Who *are* you?" he said finally.

"Just a security man who doesn't like getting shot up. And I don't like getting played. So you tell me who it was driving a black Caddy with a mask on and we'll go away friends."

He spoke with an empty voice. "I don't want you around here anymore."

"Tell me what you know," I said. "And remember, I can read your mind."

"Take him out of here," Parsons said.

"Jay J," Kat said, "do you have any idea who might have done this?"

"Of course not! I'm not some gangster! I'm a political consultant!"

I bit my tongue.

"Have you heard from her?" I said.

"No. And I don't want to. You're not going to tell anyone, are you? If this gets out, I'll never be hired again."

"I have no interest in hurting your rocketing career," I said. "But I want to know what you know about her and where she might be."

"Listen, it was just to blow off steam, you know? For both of us. She wanted it same as I did."

Kat was shaking her head like a disappointed mother.

"But I don't know anything else about her," he said. "Except that she's got issues."

"You helped her with those, no doubt," I said.

"And you're perfect, right?" he said.

"I'm a delicate flower."

Kat laughed.

Parsons put his head in his hands and rubbed his face. A washing motion, trying to remove the stain of his exposure. Guys like Parsons are all about image. On TV, on radio, saying wise things, holding up charts, looking at the future. One false move and you lose your standing. Like that guy who made his reputation during the Clinton years, then got a gig on Fox News where he excoriated the Clintons every chance he got, then predicted a whopping Romney victory in 2012, right up into election night.

Oops.

And he was gone.

Parsons had spent his productive adult years not giving away secrets, being the one to get into heads, not the other way around. It was unfamiliar territory for him. If I was the merciful type I might have felt sorry for him.

WE WALKED OUT to the street and a cold snap of bay air crunched my shoulder. It felt good and bad at the same time, like cracking your knuckles.

"Tell me, how did you know?" Kat said.

"Know what?"

"About Jay J and Leeza?"

"I'm just an amazing guy."

She shook her head "Will you please?"

"You'll be amazed when I tell you."

"Amaze me."

"Buy me a drink and I'll tell you," I said.

"Mike, you have to rest."

"I don't want to rest."

"What did the doctor tell you to do?" Kat said.

"He suggested gin," I said.

"Mike ..."

"Insisted on it, in fact."

Kat laughed. "Are you sure you're not some sort of salesman?"

"We're all selling something, aren't we?"

She didn't argue the point. Her car was in a structure next to the building. She drove us to a hotel up on Nob Hill. Dropped her car off with the valet and ushered me inside and to the right.

The bar was all art deco and low lights. A hostess in a black dress that stayed on her only by violating the laws of gravity smiled.

"Hello, Grace," Kat said.

"Nice to see you, Kat," Grace said. She gave me a look and tried to keep the smile on her face. It took effort.

"Grace," Kat said, "can you get my friend here a sport coat? The biggest one you can find."

"Of course," she said.

"You ashamed of my shirt?" I said.

"I have an image to protect," she said. "I can't be seen around town with a one-armed pharmaceutical salesman, can I?"

"Good point."

Grace came back with a big gray sport coat. She held it up so I could put my left arm through. She draped the right side over my shoulder. It was like a circus tent.

"Whose coat was this?" I said. "Oliver Hardy?"

Grace said, "Who is Oliver Hardy?"

"Just shoot me now," I said.

"Bad joke, considering," Kat said. "Come on."

The bar top was backlit onyx, like something from a Douglas Adams end-of-the-universe novel. It was almost noon and a professional crowd was starting to filter in.

The bartender was a woman who knew Kat, and they chatted. Then she introduced me. Her name was Yumiko. I shook her hand with my left.

"I guess you're not a two-fisted drinker today," Yumiko said.

"Just serve me twice as much," I said.

I ordered a double Beefeater and lime juice. Kat ordered a Royal Romance. I asked what was in a Royal Romance.

Yumiko said, "Gin, Grand Marnier, and, of course, passion fruit juice." She bobbed her eyebrows.

"And if you have three," Kat said, "you get royally messed up."

"What's your limit?" I said.

"That depends on how you treat me," she said.

She was quick, she was smart, she was knockout beautiful, especially with the amber light of the onyx bar on her face. Dionysus was kicking Apollo's butt inside me. Apollo, the rational self, was yelling instructions and reaching for water buckets. Dionysus, the body and ecstasy, was charging up hills and through walls with his toga on fire.

"Tell me about how you knew," Kat said. "Jay J is so perfect. Nobody ever gets to him the way I saw you get to him."

I said, "When I was in college, I used to do a card trick. I'd shuffle a deck of cards and then tell somebody to think of a card. Just think of it. I liked to do this with a few people around."

"And?"

"Then I'd ask the person to name the card out loud. He'd do it. I'd feel the deck and say, 'Your card is the twenty-first card from the top of the deck.' Then I'd feel it again. 'Your card is now the tenth card from the top of the deck.' I'd pause for dramatic effect."

"Of course."

"Then I'd give the deck one more feel and say, 'Believe it or not, your card is now at the very top of the deck.' And I'd turn it over."

"And it was the card?"

"Almost never. So I'd say, 'On the way to the top, your card changed to ...' whatever the card was."

"That's not a trick."

"It's a goof. But once in a great while, the actual card comes up. That happened one night in a dorm full of jocks and me, when I was the most unathletic kid since Spanky of The Little Rascals. The captain of the water polo team said the trick better be good or he'd pants me. I did the trick and his card was on top."

"What did he do?"

"He tried to pants me anyway. But a bunch of the other guys jumped him and took off *his* pants. It was a proud moment, boy."

"So you just guessed that Jay J was sleeping with her?"

"A guess and a little instinct. I caught a glance of his when I was in the office the first time. And it turns out I was right. If I'd been wrong, what would I lose? Sometimes you just take a shot."

Yumiko brought our drinks and Kat and I clinked glasses.

"Why aren't you involved with someone?" I said.

"I was, for seven years," she said. "It didn't end well."

"Happens."

"I thought he was going to be governor of California someday."

"Is all life politics to you?"

She stared into her Royal Romance. "Maybe it is."

"Why?"

She looked up. "Is this psychoanalytical or just talk?"

"You go as far as you want to," I said.

"All right." She took a sip, put the glass down. "I never thought I was any good at anything. Always less than my big sister, who was good at everything. Sports, drama, school, looks. Went to a very conservative private school."

"Where?"

"Odessa, Missouri. My parents wanted me to go to Bob Jones University, but I—"

"The Christian school?"

"Full disclosure, I'm a PK."

"What's that?"

"Preacher's kid."

I nodded.

She said, "I also applied to Georgetown. And got in. They

weren't happy about that. But that's where it all started. The place reeks of politics."

"How'd you end up working for the Dems?"

"It's just how I evolved." She gave a short, conflicted laugh.

"What's wrong?"

"Oh, it's just ironic. My parents. They don't believe in evolution. I guess I turned into their mutated spawn." This time she did not laugh. She took a thoughtful drink then came back to her story. "So anyway, I got a job in the office of Genevieve Griffin right out of college, and one thing led to another."

"Are you good at what you do?"

"Very," she said.

"What exactly is it that you do?"

"I put out fires. I start others. I make the occasional press appearance."

"And what does your big sister think of you now?"

"She thinks I'm the daughter of Satan," Kat said. "But we still talk at Christmas and Thanksgiving."

Ease back and drink your gin, Romeo. This is going way too fast. You're not the surrender-to-the-moment type, except when you get mad. Then you end up hurting the people around you, Romeo. Maybe that's all you do.

"Mike?"

"Hmm?"

"Would you like to come to my place tonight?"

I said, "That would be starting a fire."

"I know," she said. "I mean, I could take care of you. Your wound and all."

"Like *A Farewell to Arms*."

"Hemingway."

"An enduring love story. And a tragic one."

"Nobody I've ever met talks like you," she said.

"I get that a lot."

"What about you? Why aren't you attached to anyone?"

I didn't answer. She looked embarrassed. I said, "Would it be unfair of me to plead the Fifth?"

"Yes," she said.

"All right, Kat. I have a past I'm not proud of and I've hurt people. I don't like doing that."

She waited.

I said, "Sometimes I think people deserve to be hurt, and I've been trained to do that, too. But even then, it's not easy being judge, jury and ..."

"Executioner?"

"Guy who breaks other guys' bones."

"Have you ever broken a woman's bones?"

I thought of the woman I had to kill. She'd been there while my finger got sliced off. She was going to watch me get cut up into little pieces. She was bad and I ended her life.

"Don't get too close to me, Kat."

There was a pause, a feeling like in the cartoons when Elmer Fudd is out on a tree limb and has been sawing it from the wrong side and the limb breaks off and leaves Elmer hanging in mid-air, just before the harsh realization that he's over a thousand-foot cliff.

I was Fudd. Meant to be alone, not connected to other people who, if they put their arms around, me would go down, too.

I was Alcatraz. Kat was the city. That's the way it always would be. Maybe should be.

Then Kat put her hand on top of mine. No words.

"Going well I see," Yumiko said, sauntering over. "I make a good Royal Romance, don't I?"

I left my hand where it was.

For a moment.

Then I took it away.

And that's all that happened that night.

. . .

IN THE MORNING, I cleaned up my wound as best I could, then took BART over to Oakland. Sable Wilson lived near the Oakland Coliseum. I walked, getting more than a few stares. Not so much because of my skin tone but because I looked like a Civil War soldier after Shiloh. Not only was my arm was in a sling, I had a stiffness in my hip that caused a limp.

Which is why I paused to admire a pickup basketball game in a fenced-off blacktop. Five-on-five, and they were going at it like most city ballers do, as if this was an NBA playoff game. They were fast and talking smack and dialed in. It would be nice to be like that about something, anything. To have one passion and pursuit and forget everything else when you were at it. But that's not the kind of mind I have. I'm always shuffling pieces around and looking for the pattern, then trying other pieces to see if they fit just as well.

The only time I ever felt focused was in the cage, but even then I'd be thinking about the other guy, and faces in the first row, and even the ref. Pieces.

I looked down and saw a kid standing at the fence, watching. He looked at me, then back at the game.

Then I looked back at the game.

Then the kid said, "What happened to you?" He was eight or nine. He wore blue jeans, a T-shirt, and a Golden State Warriors jersey with the number 30 on it. His shoes were gray high-top Under Armours.

"I got hurt," I said.

"Playin'?"

"No, somewhere else."

"Does it hurt?"

"A little," I said. "You play?"

"Uh-huh."

"You good?"

He shrugged.

"You practice?" I said.

He nodded.

"Practice with both hands," I said. "You don't want 'em to know your weakness and overplay you."

"Where'd you play?" the kid asked.

"Just messing around," I said.

"You play pro?"

"Uh, no."

"I'm gonna."

"Yeah? For the Warriors?"

He smiled, nodded.

"Go for it," I said. "What's your name?"

"Richard."

"Mike."

He smiled.

"I've got to go, Richard. You keep practicing."

"Okay."

Maybe Richard would make it. The odds were against it, of course, but you can't let odds stop you from trying to do what you want to do. I thought of Henry then, back in L.A., and how hard it is to be a kid these days. Maybe it was harder in medieval Mongolia, but who knows? Every kid born is dealt cards and the hands are not all the same. Sometimes the cards stink, and you hope the kid has somebody in his life to get him through and teach him how to play. I had that once, right up until I was seventeen.

I walked up 85th Street to where Sable Wilson lived. The houses all along the way had iron fences in front of them. Sable's house was yellow with three cement steps in front leading to the door. Pots with geraniums, healthy and full, were on each step.

I heard a car slowing.

It was an Oakland Police cruiser. It stopped. A black patrol officer on the passenger side leaned out the window and said, "Help you?"

"No thanks," I said.

"You looking for somebody?"

"Right here," I said.

"Mind if we talk to you a minute?" He was getting out of the car now, and so was his partner, a trimmer version of the first.

"You live around here?" The first cop said. His nameplate said *Charles*. His partner stood at the rear of the patrol car, watching.

"No, just visiting."

"Mind telling us who?"

"Well, I do, yes."

"You have some ID on you?"

"Sure."

He waited.

"May I see it?" he said.

"Nope," I said.

"Let me see some identification, please."

"No."

Officer Charles frowned. "Why you making this hard?"

"I have this thing about privacy. Like it's a right guaranteed to me under the Constitution. And since you have no cause to detain me, this conversation is purely voluntary on my part, right?"

"We just like to keep an eye on things" he said.

"You don't have to worry about me. I was in an accident and my arm hurts. So I'm snappish."

"Snappish?"

"Bilious."

"What?"

"In an ill humor."

Charles frowned. "Have you been drinking alcohol, sir, or taking drugs?"

I said, "You think I'm intoxicated?"

"Tell you the truth, you sound a little strange," he said.

"It's my manner, sir," I said, quoting Peter O'Toole in *Lawrence of Arabia.* "And now I have some business to attend to."

His partner said, "Let's go."

Charles said, "See to your business then. Just be careful around here."

He emphasized his warning with a slight nod and a squint.

"I appreciate the job you're doing, Officer Charles," I said.

The two policemen got back in their cruiser and left.

THERE WAS NO answer when I knocked. I tried again. Nothing.

I sat on the top step and looked at the geraniums. Deep-red like a fine claret. Robust petals. A hearty breed for this time of year. I like flowers that survive. Tough. Your begonias and black-eyed Susans, your bush daisies and marigolds. Taking the heat and refusing to wither. My mom was like that.

"Young man?"

A woman stood at the fence of the neighboring house. She was rotund, elderly. But also a hearty breed. Her bearing said she was not to be trifled with.

I stood and walked to the fence.

"I'm waiting for Sable Wilson," I said.

"Is she expecting you?"

"No. I met her the other night. At church."

"You go to Temple Baptist?"

"No, ma'am. In San Francisco. There was a rally."

She raised her eyebrows. "The one with the smoke?"

"That's the one. I met Mrs. Wilson outside. We had a nice little talk."

"Did you get hurt there?" she said.

"No, after," I said.

"Are you a police officer?"

"Far from it."

"Are you a reporter?"

"No, ma'am."

"Well then, Sable helps out at the church kitchen some mornings. I expect her back soon."

I said, "Can I be right upfront with you, Ms. ..."

"McKinney. Mrs. Arthela McKinney."

"Call me Mike. I was working as security at the church. I saw Mrs. Wilson there with a younger woman."

"T'Kia," Mrs. McKinney said. "Her granddaughter."

"Ah."

"She was on the news, you know."

"I saw it."

"Mm-hm." She looked down.

"What is it?" I said.

She shook her head. "I just don't know. That T'Kia's been trouble for Sable. Trouble to herself. I don't trust that girl."

"Do you think she's lying about all this?"

"Wouldn't be the first time," Mrs. McKinney said, "And I don't like that lawyer of hers, whatever her name is."

"What does Sable think?"

"I haven't talked to her about it. I think it makes her sad."

"Does her granddaughter live with her?"

"Moved out last year, went to the city. Girl like that doesn't belong in the city all alone."

A man's voice bellowed, "Arthela! Come on in here now."

He was standing on the steps of the McKinney house in a white T-shirt and slacks and slippers. He had a newspaper folded in one hand.

Mrs. McKinney turned to him. "I'm having a talk, dear."

"Come in now," he said.

"What's got into you?" she said.

"Nothing's got into me that I don't want there, and I want you to come on in now."

Mrs. McKinney turned back to me. "I don't know why that man is making all that noise."

"I think he wants you to come in," I said with a smile.

"You think so?" She winked at me. "You watch. He'll be coming over here next."

"Arthela!"

To me she said, "Just keep talking, young man."

"I don't want to cause any trouble," I said.

"We need a little trouble every now and then. Spices up a marriage."

Sure enough, the man came up to the fence and said to me, "Go on now."

"Oscar!" Arthela McKinney said. "You behave yourself. This here's a guest of Sable's."

"He doesn't look like a guest," Oscar said. "I had to chase one of 'em off the other day, hanging around."

"What are you talking about, Oscar?"

"He knows," Oscar said, looking me in the eye. "Don't you?"

I said, "I'm afraid not."

"Bothering Sable, checking out her house," Oscar said. "Two of 'em. I got my rifle."

"You did *not*!" Arthela McKinney said.

"Don't think I didn't," Oscar said.

"Sir," I said, "I want to assure you I'm not connected with the people that may have done that."

"Couple of kids, stringy-hair kids up to no good."

"Mr. McKinney," I said, "can you describe these kids?"

"I just told you. You know 'em, don't you?"

"The odds are I don't. But—"

"Yeah! You see!"

"Mr. McKinney, tell me what you can about them."

"Why should I?"

"Tell him, Oscar."

"You stay out of this—"

"Oscar O'Dell McKinney, you tell this young man what he wants to hear, and don't you make me mad now, hear?"

Oscar O'Dell McKinney issued a championship grumble, then slapped his leg with the newspaper. "All I saw was stringy hair, like I said. One was kinda tall and skinny, and one was kinda short and roly poly. They were walking up and down in front of Sable's, and I don't mind telling you they didn't exactly look like they belonged here. So I came out with my carbine and I tell'em to shove off."

"Oscar, you never told me that."

"I didn't want to worry you. You were at the hospital that night." To me he said proudly, "She volunteers down at the hospital, sitting with all the little mothers."

"Your rifle!" Arthela said. "The idea!"

"They were up to no good," Oscar said. "Just like I don't know why this boy is here."

"I think I do know those fellas," I said.

"Okay then!" Oscar said.

"They jumped me. When I first got to the city. They attacked me."

"You don't say it," Arthela McKinney said.

Oscar McKinney scowled. "I want to know what is going on, and I want to know it now."

"Sir, I don't know just yet, but I'm going to find out."

"Here comes Sable," Mrs. McKinney said.

Sable Wilson was walking toward us, dressed in what her generation called go-to-meeting clothes. A blue ensemble, complete with hat. She saw us standing there and quickened her step.

"Why hello," she said to me. "How on earth ..."

"You know this man, Sable?" Oscar said.

"Yes I do. His name is Mike."

"Well I'll just be," Oscar said.

"Yes, you will," Arthela said. "Let's go back inside."

"Pleased to meet you," I said.

Oscar frowned. Arthela took him by the arm and led him back to the house. I felt a new appreciation for the institution of marriage and the role of the wife as keeper of her husband.

"Mike," Sable said, "what are you doing here?"

"Can we talk inside?"

"Of course. But how did you know where I lived?"

"The internet."

She shook her head. "I don't like that at all."

"Will you forgive me? I needed to talk to you."

Sable Wilson gave me a look full of what her generation called Christian charity.

"Come in," she said.

I followed her up the steps.

"Love your geraniums," I said.

"Oh, you know flowers?"

"A hobby of mine. They're one of the few honest things left on earth."

"How you do talk." She smiled, unlocked her front door, and in we went.

I felt an immediate warmth in the place, as if it had been lovingly preserved from an earlier time when people treated each other as neighbors and guests were welcome any time. We were in the small living room. The sofa might have seen better days, but that was the point—they were better. Over the sofa was a framed needlework saying: *Lord, make me an instrument of thy peace.*

Sable offered me tea and I said yes, and she hummed softly in the kitchen as I sat in the living room. There was a little booklet on the coffee table. *Our Daily Bread.* I picked it up and opened it at random. There was a Bible verse that read: *Just as you want men to do to you, you also do to them likewise.*

Now that was a coincidence. My rule is '*Do unto them before they do unto you.*'

I hoped Jesus wouldn't mind.

Sable came in to join me. "The water's boiling. I must say I am surprised to see you again, Mike. How did you hurt your arm?"

"It's my shoulder. Somebody tried to kill me."

"Oh my Jesus."

"Not long after the meeting broke up. The smoke bomb."

She folded her hands in her lap and looked at them.

"Your granddaughter," I said.

She looked up. "You know about her?"

"I saw her on the news. She's making a claim about Samuel Johnson."

"I don't know why."

"You don't believe it's true?"

"I don't know what to believe with T'Kia. I tried so hard. Her mother died, you know. I raised T'Kia by myself. I tried so hard ..."

I waited.

She said, "That Samuel Johnson seems decent, but I guess you can't tell from just looking."

"Do you know where I might find T'Kia?"

"Why?"

"I'd like to talk to her myself."

"I don't know as she'll talk to anyone now. She told me, at the meeting she told me she was going away for a while and not to try to find her."

"Did she say why?"

Sable shook her head. "But they must have her, that lawyer and all. I don't like her one bit."

"The lawyer?"

"That woman is a troublemaker," Sable said.

The kettle whistled in the kitchen. Sable got up, wearily, and made her way there. This time there was no humming.

And then I heard something crash.

I ran to the kitchen and saw broken cups on the floor and Sable with her head in her hands, shaking.

There I stood for a moment in time, realizing without analyzing that I had never in my life physically comforted another human being. Never put my arm around a troubled friend's shoulder. I had no close friends. When you're fourteen and going to Yale, you're a bit of a freak. I never had a pet. My pets were books. You don't comfort books, they comfort you.

I thought I should turn around and not profane this fine house with who I am and what I bring about.

And then the moment passed as evanescent as an eye-blink, and I wrapped my left arm around Sable Wilson and pulled her to me. She wept into my chest and I held her there and put my head on her hair and we stayed that way for a long time.

LATER IN THE living room, as we had our tea, she said, "Do you believe in God, Mike?"

"To be perfectly honest with you, Sable, I'm on the fence."

"Time to get offa that fence."

"I do think about such things, though," I said. "You can trust me on that."

"You keep thinking," she said with a smile. "Time'll come when you can move from thinking to trusting. When it does, off the fence."

"Deal," I said.

Sable took a sip of tea with perfect etiquette—sitting up straight, index finger through the cup handle and thumb on top of the handle to secure it. Her three remaining fingers curved underneath. No pinkie extension, which is rude and cartoony. My mother taught me this. It made me glad I made the trip out here.

She put the cup down on the saucer. "There is one friend T'Kia has," she said. "Her name is Roberta. If anyone would know where T'Kia is, it would be Roberta."

"Can I get in touch with Roberta?" I said.

"I believe she works at the Target up in Emeryville."

"That's not too far," I said. "But I'm on foot."

"Would you like to drive my car?" Sable said.

"You would let me?"

"I don't drive much. Don't trust my eyes. But it still runs."

"I would be happy to drive your car."

"Can you do it? With your arm and all?"

"As long as I don't have to make a U-turn."

"Then let's go."

"You're coming?"

"Roberta knows me. She doesn't know you. I think I better come along."

SABLE'S CAR WAS a Buick with one hundred and seven thousand miles on it. I took off my sling to drive. Sable remarked that I looked like I was in pain and I told her that this was my regular face. She guided me through the streets of Oakland all the way to Emeryville.

The Target looked like every other Target I've ever seen. Corporate America doing its job to attract and keep the never-ending supply of consumers filtering through like a river of profit, which is not a bad thing. It gives people jobs, like the young woman we were looking for. It keeps people off the streets. It keeps people distracted with goods and foods and lust for things, which is better than lust for blood or thy neighbor's wife. Yes, Target, one of our temples, like Best Buy or Hooters.

Sable and I found Roberta in the toy section. She was stocking a shelf with dolls. The doll boxes were on top of a cart. Roberta wore the red vest of her employment and the blank look of her task. When she saw Sable and me she almost dropped a Barbie.

"Hello, Roberta," Sable said.

"What are you doing here?"

"Honey, can you tell me where T'Kia is? We need to talk to her."

Roberta eyed me suspiciously "Who's he?"

"He's not police," Sable said. "He's a friend."

Roberta did not look convinced.

"I think she's in trouble," I said. "I work for the campaign."

"She's in no trouble except from people wanting to get at her," Roberta said.

"Is that what she says?" I asked.

"I don't know," Roberta said.

"When did you last talk to her?"

"I can't be talking to you now."

Sable said, "Please, honey."

Roberta shook her head. "She wouldn't like that. You and her don't get along."

"That's our family business, don't you think?"

Roberta said nothing. She put another doll on the shelf.

"She won't answer me on the phone," Sable said.

"Nobody's supposed to know where she is," Roberta said.

"But you know," I said.

"I didn't say that."

"Well, do you?" I said.

She looked at the Barbies. The Barbies looked at her.

"It's just to talk," I said. "If they're making her say something she doesn't want to say, she could be in real trouble."

"She's got a lawyer," Roberta said.

"Do you know who that lawyer is?" I said.

Roberta nodded.

"Doesn't she strike you as the kind of lawyer who likes publicity, and a lot of it?"

Roberta shrugged. "T'Kia knows what she's doing."

Sable said, "Please give us a chance. I've known you practically your whole life, Roberta. How many times've you been over to my house? How many times did I feed you?"

Roberta looked at the Barbie in her hands.

"Do you ever think I'd do anything that would hurt my baby?" Sable said.

"You're going to talk God to her," Roberta said.

"Not this time," Sable said. "I just need to know."

Roberta gave me another quick scan. "You gonna tell anybody? Reporters?"

"Why would I do that?" Sable said.

"What about him?"

"You can trust me, Roberta," I said.

"I don't know you."

"But you know me, honey," Sable said. "You know I don't lie. You know I know good people. This is good people here."

With a resigned gesture, Roberta placed another Barbie on the shelf. "I think she's afraid," Roberta said.

"Of what?" I said.

"Things happening so fast. But she knows what she's doing."

"What do you mean by that?" Sable asked.

Roberta said, "She's gonna get more money out of that lawyer. Lawyer thinks T'Kia's gonna be good with scraps, she got another think coming."

I said, "What's she going to do to get more money?"

"That's all I know," Roberta said. "I got to get—"

"Is she in the city?"

"I'm not supposed to tell. She wasn't even supposed to tell me. But ..."

"It's all right, honey," Sable said.

Roberta said, "She wants me to come, to hang out with her. She's gonna be there a long time."

"When were you going to see her?" I said.

"Saturday," Roberta said.

"Where?" Sable said. "Please, honey, please."

After a long pause, Roberta took out her phone and read us an address.

"Do you know if she's there alone?" I said.

"Huh?"

"Do they have people with her?" I said.

"T'Kia doesn't like that. But she's not supposed to go out."

"Roberta, will you promise me something?" I said.

"What?"

"Give us two days. Don't tell T'Kia about this until we have a chance to talk to her."

Roberta said, "But what are you gonna talk to her *about*?"

"Trust me, won't you?" Sable said.

Roberta closed her eyes. Then she nodded.

I DID A little shopping before we left. I bought a hair visor, graycolored, the kind with fake gray tufts sticking up. Then some sunglasses and a XXL 49ers sweatshirt.

In the car going back to Sable's, I asked her about T'Kia's personality.

"She's strong-willed, that's for sure," Sable said. "Defiant, you might say."

"Did you see her on the news?"

"I saw it. She was scared."

"But would she do what they tell her to?"

"Depends. If she knows she's going to get something. She was always trying to scam her old grandmama. I had to stay one jump ahead of her." She paused. "We had words, about a year ago, she wasn't going to church anymore and she wasn't going back to school. I told her those were my conditions and if she didn't like that she would have to leave. She left. I don't know if I did right."

"You did right," I said. "Your kind of love is rare."

She looked out the window then, and I got the feeling she was trying not to cry.

I TOOK BART back to the city and called Ira.

"Mike, what's been happening up there?"

"I'm meeting all sorts of nice people."

"And?"

"I know where the woman is, the one making the charge against Johnson."

"Holy cow," Ira said.

"She's in hiding," I said.

"Now what?"

"I talk to her."

"How?" Ira said. "She'll have people around."

"I'll pick my spot," I said. "And I have a hole card—her grandmother, who raised her."

"How did you swing that?"

"I swing, that's what I do. Something else came up. Something I can't put together. Those two guys who jumped me when I got here?"

"Yeah?"

"They were in an Oakland neighborhood some days before that. They were scoping out the house of T'Kia Wilson's grandmother."

"What's the connection?"

"I don't know. It doesn't make sense. But the cosmos does not use loaded dice."

"I'm more concerned with the crap game you're playing in San Francisco."

I said, "The key to it all may be this girl they tried to kill, Leeza. But she's gone."

Ira said, "Can you find her?"

"I know where she lives," I said. "But she'd be stupid to go back there. I don't think she's stupid. She just lacks certain social graces."

"Give Uncle Ira as much info as you can."

I gave him what I knew about Leeza Edgar, which was not much.

"One more thing," I said. "Kat Hogg."

"Yes?"

"It's getting a little complicated."

"Oh no."

"Just a little."

"Like Tristan and Isolde?"

"No, no love potion. Just a friendly drink. I do think she kind of likes me."

"What is this, middle school?" Ira said.

"You want to know what's going on, or don't you?"

"All right," Ira said. "Do you like her?"

"I'm not going to ask her to the dance or anything."

"Didn't answer my question."

"Didn't intend to."

"Your mind is a terrible thing to waste," Ira said. "Keep it on your job."

THE PLACE ROBERTA gave up was a nondescript apartment building just off of Van Ness. There was a laundry on the right and a pizza place on the left. It was two stories and set back a little from the street. I'd left my sling in my hotel room. In my shades and visor and Niner sweatshirt I was just another San Francisco citizen. Maybe one of the more normal looking ones.

I watched the place for a while from across the street. There were two ways they could play this. If they were keeping T'Kia Wilson under wraps in there, they wouldn't want too much commotion. Still, they'd probably have a bodyguard or handler with her, despite what Roberta thought.

But then again, if T'Kia was strong-willed, like Sable said, maybe she might have worked it so she'd have lots of alone time.

There was only one way to find out.

I went to the pizza place and ordered a small and had them put it in a box. I came outside and waited until somebody came out of the apartment doors. It was a young guy, and when I ran up holding the pizza box like a waiter with a tray, he held the door for me.

"Looks good," the guy said.

"Is good," I said. "We deliver."

"Nice lid," he said, looking at my hair hat.

There was a security camera in the lobby. I did my best pizza delivery pose and went to the elevator and then up to the second floor. The pizza smelled good. I found the apartment Roberta had named for us.

Knocked.

Nothing.

I knocked again.

"Pizza," I said. "From Sable."

Nothing. No sense of movement inside. She could have been asleep. And I could have had unlimited time, but didn't.

Your ficus tree can learn to pick an old lock. You can get

"home for the turn" with a paper clip and wrench. If you don't have a wrench, you can improvise.

I carried my pizza to the far end of the corridor and took the stairs down to the first floor. There was a back door with a push bar. I went outside to a small alley. I ripped off a chunk of pizza box and wedged it into the door. Then I tossed a perfectly nice pie into a Dumpster.

On my phone I found a hardware store five blocks away. I was careful not to bump into anybody. My shoulder throbbed and one good knock was going to get an attention-grabbing wail from me. No one in San Francisco wants to see a 49er yelp unless they lose to the Seahawks.

In the store, I went to the checkout line where they had candy and smaller items. I picked out a box of large paperclips. I borrowed one. I took up a box of smalls and borrowed a couple of those.

I put the boxes back.

Then I went to the tools section and found the needle-nose pliers. I took out my large paper clip and unbent one of the sides. Then with the pliers I made a small bend at the end, then another small bend. The needle-nose pliers worked very well. I applied the same technique on a smaller clip, making one little bend at the end and then another to the side.

I owed the store something, so I bought a pack of Juicy Fruit at the counter. The young woman at the cash register said, "Did you find everything you need?"

"Oh yes. The Juicy Fruit is especially ripe this time of year."

She did not laugh. Or smile. I paid with two singles and got back less change than I thought I would. The price of gum had gone up since I was a kid. I did not stick around to complain.

I got back to the alley and apartment's rear door. My wedge was still there.

Up the stairs and back to the corridor I went.

So far, I'd seen no one inside the building. I could hear

some jazz coming from the apartment to my immediate right. Billie Holliday. Good taste. People listening to the blues usually weren't in any hurry to go anywhere.

But I would have to act fast.

The large paperclip I had fashioned into a tension wrench for picking a lock. The small paperclip with the bend at the end was the picker proper. The other clip I used to rake the bottom of the tumblers. The last time I'd done this was twenty years ago to get into a lab at Yale. They didn't even use Yale locks.

One by one the tumblers clicked and the paperclip tension wrench turned the latch and the door opened.

I went in and closed it quickly behind me.

No lights on in the place and no light coming in from windows. I was flying on the edge of total recklessness, of course. Felony breaking and entering. But at this point I was channeling my inner Nietzsche and making my own reality. Getting your finger cut off and sewed back on, and getting shot in the shoulder so you feel like a wounded elephant, is clarifying. It makes you feel you've got nothing much left to lose.

Who knew how much time I had before someone showed up here? But then again, who knows how much time we have on earth? This is how your mind works when you decide to do something really daring or really stupid. But if I got nicked, I was ready with a story that would blow up Jay J. Parsons and the whole campaign with it. I was betting I could talk enough blarney that the powers-that-be would not think it worth the trouble to press charges. I knew how they thought better than they did.

Now it was a matter of keeping my fingerprints off anything while I snooped around. If T'Kia came in, I'd pull the Sable card and tell her she sent me. I'd show her her grandmother's car keys. If there was a bodyguard with her, I'd hit him with my left hand and leave.

The apartment was spare. It was a hideout apartment, not a real living space. There was, in a nice ironical twist, a pizza box from the place next door on the dining table. It was as if I really had delivered the thing, and I counted that as a good sign.

Nothing else in the living room showed much sign of life.

In the kitchen were some unwashed dishes in the sink and an open Red Bull can.

I went through the other kitchen entrance and down the hall. Bathroom on the right. Open door to the bedroom at the end.

At the door I smelled something foul.

And then I saw the source.

She was lying on top of the bed in her own filth. I didn't have to look twice to know she was dead.

I CIRCLED AROUND the bed, slowly, careful not to touch anything or step in anything. There was no blood, so I figured on strangulation or asphyxiation. I took a closer look and saw a darkening around her neck. It was rough but uniform, definitely strangulation with some kind of cloth. Not a rope, which would have been a thinner ligature mark. Not hands, which would've left deeper spots where the thumbs pressed.

Her head lolled to one side and her eyes had the bloodshot look that comes with ruptured capillaries caused by strangulation. Her right arm was against her side. Her left arm crooked at the elbow in a right angle. Her left fist was closed around something. I bent over to look at it. It was paper of some kind. Her fingers were not entirely enclosed around it, giving the appearance of holding the thing loosely. It looked like it could have been planted.

Which of course meant I took it.

It was a business card, slightly crumpled. I straightened it out. It said:

Samuel Johnson
    Prof. of Economics
    UCLA

That's when the sweat stains started. I had to get out of there. Someone was going to be coming to this apartment because whoever killed her was going to report to the cops that she was missing, and the last known residence was right here. They would come because this was a setup, clumsy as it was, to plant this business card in her hand. That would be enough to dominate the rest of the campaign. The death of T'Kia Wilson alone might've been enough. But the card would mean raw meat for the newshounds.

I put the card in my pocket and went to the door. I looked out the peephole and didn't see anyone in the corridor as far as I could tell. I put my hand under my T-shirt and opened the door with it, a crack, and check the corridor again. Empty.

Out the door and back down the stairs. Had I been Jason on the Argo, I would've thought Zeus was smiling favorably on me. I went out the pushed door into the alley and thought, *No one has seen me.*

And then I heard a voice. "I seen you."

It was an old derelict. He was dressed in brown clothes that at one time had been red or white. His face was equally brown with dirt, but at least his teeth, yellow and orange, gave him a festive variety. Of course he didn't have all his teeth.

"What have you seen?" I said.

"I know what you did."

"Tell me."

"Not till you give me some."

"Some what?"

"Some of what you got."

His breath was strong enough to break a knee on.

"How would you like this hat?" I said.

He looked at me and his beady eyes got ping-pong-ball size. "That'll do," he said.

I handed over the visor. His eyes got wider. "That's your hair!"

"Now it's your hair," I said.

He put it on and wheezed out a laugh.

"So tell me what I did," I said.

"Huh? Oh, uh, don't remember."

"Then don't tell anybody," I said.

"Tell'em what?"

"What you don't remember."

"Whu?"

"But just so you know ..."

"Uh?"

"I didn't do it."

"Do what?"

"Exactly."

His eyes seemed to cross.

I gave him a nod and walked away. I hoped he would keep the hat on, and I hoped the cops would find him out back with it. And then he could try to convince them that somebody gave it to him. And the cops would think sure, that's what a killer would do, talk face-to-face with a card-carrying member of the dregs of society and leave a clue with him.

I walked down Van Ness, then to California, trying to keep my right arm from swaying. I'd need to change the bandages and all that soon. I'd need help. I'd need Kat.

Kat. Was it possible that she knew about this? Was it at all thinkable? That in some back room she'd overheard a whisper?

She would not have been directly involved. Why not? How well do you know her, Romeo? That's not being rational, boy. Don't let Eros have his way with you now. I stopped in a thrift store and bought a couple of shirts. I paid for them then went in the back and put one on. It was a 60s retro with surfboards and woodies and palm trees on it. I rolled up the Niner sweatshirt and stuffed it in a street trash receptacle a few blocks away.

BACK IN MY hotel room, flopped on the bed, I studied the peeling wallpaper. Geese. Happy flying geese. No hunters with shotguns. All was perfect. I thought of the things happening that didn't make sense, didn't fit into a pattern like the geese on the walls.

I wanted to go to Sable, to prepare her for the news, to hold her again when she cried. But I couldn't do that. The cops would be out to talk to her and if she knew what I knew, she'd have to tell them.

With effort I took my shirt off. The back of it was stained from the seeping of the bandages. Now I wish I'd reconsidered having Kat with me. But I didn't want her just to play nurse. Which was why I was alone in the first place.

I'm good at not having people around me.

Best skill. Would look great on a résumé and sound terrific in an interview. *Can you operate a forklift? No. What can you do? Stay away from people. Why would you do that? Because it's best all around.*

In the bathroom I turned around enough to see the bandages in the mirror. A brownish-yellow glaze was forming on the outside. The pain was really kicking in now. I couldn't lift my right arm without all the nerves joining in an angry chorus of *Don't Do Me Like That.*

So I did a little cleaning up with the creative use of a hand towel.

Then I called Ira.

"How's the wound?" he said.

"It'll heal," I said.

"Time wounds all heels," Ira said. "I think Groucho Marx said that."

"What did he say about finding a dead body?"

"I don't recall him ... Oh no. Who?"

"Samuel Johnson's phantom paramour."

"T'Kia Wilson?" Ira said.

"A messy little hit, intended to look messy," I said.

"Where? How?"

I gave him the story.

"Such a ham-fisted setup," I said. "That business card would have dominated the news. It's going to be bad for Johnson, anyway. Better have Steadman try to get ahead of this thing."

"He's a slick one," Ira said.

"You're slick too, Ira," I said.

"I prefer level-headed. Give me the address of the building where you found the girl."

I did.

"What are you going to do now?" Ira said.

"Take a shower."

"You know what I mean!"

"See the sights. Maybe take a tour of Alcatraz."

"Mike—"

"Good-night, Ira."

I THOUGHT I heard a knock on my door. I went to the peep

hole and looked out and saw nothing. I turned away and heard another knock. I opened the door.

And looked down.

He was about three and a half feet tall. A regular Hobbit. But he had the kick of a mule, and his little cowboy-booted foot knocked the door back and me with it.

And then he was inside, slamming the door behind him, and pulling out a 9mm handgun which, compared to him, looked like a cannon.

"Don't move," he said.

I almost laughed, but my mouth just hung open. Was I in Alice in Wonderland here? Was the world tipping on its crazy axis? Maybe I was in some pain-induced bad dream.

"What are you going to do?" I said. "Shoot me in the kneecap?"

"I don't like short people jokes," he said. His head was a little too large for his frame, a weather-beaten face with a jutting chin. He wore blue jeans over his boots and a red flannel shirt. How he packed his heat was a mystery. It looked like it would pull him over by its weight.

"I will do damage to you if you try to make a move," he said. "It would be a mistake to think I won't." He backed away to put more space between us. "Sit down in that chair."

I sat in the one straight-back chair that came with the room.

"Who are you?" I said.

"I'll be asking the questions."

"Please don't tell me you work for Mr. Big."

His jaw, the largest part of him, twitched. "I told you I don't like short jokes!"

"I'll be here all week," I said. "Tip the waiter on the way out."

"Shut up!"

I shrugged.

"I'm going to search the place," he said.

"Take whatever you want."

"Don't think I won't."

"I'm through thinking for the night. If you tell me what you want, maybe I can help."

"I'll make this short and sweet."

I bit my tongue.

"You're a problem," he said. "I'm going to need you to tie yourself up."

I sighed. "Look, friend, I've already been shot this week. I'm at my limit."

He studied me for a moment. "Who shot you?"

"I'd love to find out."

"Why'd you get shot?"

"I'd love to find that out, too."

"I'll tell you why you got shot. You're a scum-sucking thief and a liar."

"I am not scum-sucking."

"You've got a mouth on you, too. I hate that."

"Hate cannot drive out hate," I said. "Only love can do that."

"Huh?"

"The Reverend Dr. Martin Luther King."

He blinked. "Tie yourself up."

"With what?"

He looked around the room.

"You have any rope?" he said.

"No."

"Duct tape?"

"No."

"Wire?"

"This isn't your night, is it?" I said.

"Lie down on the floor. Face down."

"Now look—"

"Now!" He waggled his cannon at me. I wondered then if his fingers could reach the trigger. I decided not to test the theory.

I slipped off the chair and, with a little effort, put my face on the carpet. I heard the little fella padding around the room, opening the drawers of the desk, which held only a Gideon Bible and a guide to San Francisco tourist spots.

"You better hope I find it," he said.

What did he hope to find? I had no records or journals. I had only the clothes in my duffel bag and some money in my wallet. But he didn't seem interested in money. If he was going to rob me that would have been the first thing he asked for.

"The bathroom," he said. "Crawl to the bathroom."

"Dude, I'm shot up."

"Walk on your knees."

I got into that ridiculous position. "Hey, now we can speak face-to-face."

"I'm not gonna take that from you!"

"How about I crab crawl, okay?"

"Like what?"

"You know, on my butt." I used my left hand for leverage and swung my legs around and just kept them going. With my left foot I kicked his gun hand outward and with my right foot kicked him in the stomach. He fell backward and I rolled forward and got to my feet. I stepped on his wrist and pinned it to the floor. I took the gun out of his hand.

He shrieked and kicked at me with his boots. I gave his melon a healthy stomp with my shoe. Just enough to stun him. Then I ejected the magazine and thumbed out five rounds onto the bed. With some effort and more than a little pain, I took out the round in the chamber. Then I went to my second story window, opened it and threw the bullets into the night.

The little intruder was bleeding from the nose and groaning. I went to the bathroom and wet the only towel in the place, brought it back and gave it to him. By this time he was in a sitting position. He swiped the towel out of my hand and rubbed his face.

"Why'd you have to do that?" he said.

"You're kidding, right?"

"I just wanted to search the place."

"Well maybe I don't like people doing that, okay? Is that all right with you?"

He rubbed his prominent chin. "You kicked me."

I sat on the bed. "Now, suppose you tell me who you are, who you work for and what this is about."

"Don't play dumb," he said.

"Now listen, junior," I said, bobbing the gun in my left hand. "I can get a little angry myself. I have an inner Achilles."

"What?"

"The wrath of Achilles."

He looked me over. "You sound like a weird guy. Can I have my gun?"

"You're a cheeky devil."

"That cost me a lot of money."

"I'm only going to ask you one more time," I said. "Why are you here?"

"What are you going to do to me?" He rubbed his temples.

"I'm going to get the information I want or make a basketball out of you."

"You going to torture me?"

"You're torturing *me*. Can't you answer a direct question?"

He paused, giving his face one more swipe with the towel.

Then he threw the towel at me.

It got me in the face.

And then the homunculus was at the door, opening it, and zipping out into the hall.

I threw the gun and the towel on the bed and went after him.

. . .

I CAUGHT HIM at the end of the hall. His little legs were moving as fast as his physicality would allow, and when I picked him up by the back of his pants, the legs continued to run in the air. I held him away from me with my good arm as if he were a shark I'd just hooked. It would snap and thrash, but as long as I held him at arm's length, no problem.

I started walking him back to the room.

He screamed. "Help! Help!"

"Shut up."

"Help!"

I whacked him against the wall, face first. A sound came out of his throat like, *Uhhhhh.*

A door opened, the one next to mine, and an old geezer face with three days' worth of gray stubble peeked out.

"Nothing to see here," I said.

He gave one look at the stunned homunculus I was holding and quickly withdrew. Back in my room I put the little guy on the floor face down and then my knee on top.

"Just kill me why don't you?" he said.

"I don't want to kill anybody," I said.

"Yeah you do. I know all about you."

"Who told you all about me?"

He said nothing.

"Humor me. I might let you go."

"You know who it is, and he wants the money."

"I'm supposed to have money?"

"Let me up."

"Not yet. What kind of money we talking about?"

"The money you stole, man. You can't keep trying to hide."

I took my knee off him and sat in the chair. He got up like a disgruntled elf and felt his head. "Why'd you have to do that to me?"

"Listen to me, and carefully, okay?"

He looked at me blankly. I gave his cheek a little slap.

"Hey!" he said.

"Have I got your attention?" I said.

"You got it, you got it."

"I am not the guy you're looking for."

He frowned. "Yeah you are."

"I don't have any money, I didn't steal any money. I'm from L.A. I just got up here a few days ago."

"Wha ..."

"That's what I'm telling you. Who do you think I am?"

"Your name's not Ripley?"

"No, my name's not Ripley."

"I was told Ripley was in 208. I have it here." He pulled a piece of paper from his back pocket and showed it to me.

"You write this?" I said.

"No, it was given to me."

"This looks like it might say 203," I said. "Whoever wrote it got a little carried away with the last loop."

The little man snatched the paper back from me. He staggered, fell backward like he was fainting, then bounced off the side of the bed into a standing position. "Oh no," he said.

"Who hired you?" I said.

He shook his heavy head. "I don't believe this is happening. I don't believe I messed up like this."

"It happens all the time," I said.

"No, man, it's bad."

"Life is bad. It's how we handle it that counts." I couldn't believe I was counseling a gun-toting short person in the nuances of Stoic philosophy. "Why don't you tell me what this is about."

HIS NAME WAS Urban Rosetta and he was working for a

man named Cedric Wincher. All I could get out of him was that Wincher was a local crew operator and not a nice man. He'd organized a transport heist and some of the money that was his was taken by this guy Ripley. Almost a hundred grand.

Urban Rosetta owed Wincher a debt. He was a little obscure on how the debt was garnered, but I got the impression it had to do with betting on the horses.

"He gave me this job, this one job, and if I come through, I'm clear," Urban Rosetta said.

"What happens if you don't?"

"I don't even want to think about it."

"You have family, Urban?"

"My mother is all," he said.

"A mother is a lot. Where is she?"

"Petaluma."

"You see her much?" I said.

"I send her money," he said. "She doesn't know where it comes from. She thinks I'm a handyman."

I thought about what I was about to do, and a thousand voices inside me shouted that I should just let Urban Rosetta go on his way, take care of his business. I was not involved in this, didn't need to be. Shouldn't be.

I can't say to this day why I said it. It certainly didn't come from Apollo, my mind, or Dionysus, my body. Wherever it came from, I found myself saying, "Let's go talk to the guy in 203."

My shoulder was still blazing but I got a shirt on. I gave Urban his gun back, told him there would be no shooting tonight. Everything was better, I explained to him, if you can do it without a gun.

We went down the hall to 203. I stood with my back against the wall and had Urban knock. A few seconds later a voice went, "Who is it?"

Urban said, "Rent's due."

Pause. "I'm paid up."

"Not what it says here."

I was imagining the guy behind the door straining to see little Urban Rosetta through the peephole. One advantage Urban had was that people would not perceive him as any kind of threat.

The door opened and the man inside told Urban to go away, which is when I stepped around and pushed the door open. Urban scurried inside and I followed, closing the door behind me.

"Hey!" the man said. He was in a white T-shirt over khaki slacks. Bare feet. His hair was black and thick and slicked down. He was forty or so.

"Hello, Ripley," Urban Rosetta said.

"What is this?" Ripley said.

"I'll tell you what it is, punk—"

I said, "Urb, hold on a second." I was going to play good cop here, even though Urban's bad cop was more comic relief than threat.

"Who are you?" Ripley said. "Get out of my—"

"Relax," I said.

Ripley's hands went behind his back, which could mean only one thing. I'd been waiting for it, though, and left jabbed him. Down he went. Urban jumped on him like a mother monkey attacking a lion. But I have to hand it to the little guy —he came up with a .38 revolver in his hands.

He stepped back and pointed it at Ripley's head. "Now you're gonna listen."

"Easy, Urb," I said.

Then he turned the gun on me. "You're through here."

"Are you kidding me?" I said. "You point a gun at me again? I ought to feed you to the squids at the aquarium."

The .38 trembled a little in his hands. "I'm doing the talking here."

"Urban, it's not even loaded."

I had no idea if it was loaded. I just wanted Urb's momentary hesitation. When his eyes flicked down at the gun I snatched it from him. My hand speed was still a thing of beauty.

Urban Rosetta cried out pitifully.

I turned back to Ripley.

He was coming at me with a knife.

Fighting off a knife attack is hard enough with two hands. With no hands, it's impossible. Which always takes me a little longer.

My right hand was useless and I held a .38 by the barrel in my left. I spun counter-clockwise forty-five degrees, which is the first move for a close-up knife thrust coming at you. I would have grabbed his wrist with my left hand, but it was full of metal. So I used the gun as a hammer. I made less than full contact.

Ripley wasn't a pro with the blade. A pro would have come up at me with a backhand slash. Instead he pulled his hand back to prepare another thrust.

His mistake.

I fended it off with the gun butt. The .38 was now my shield. Thrust and parry. Thrust and parry. Inigo Montoya against the Dread Pirate Roberts. The clank of steel on steel.

Where was Urban?

I gave one try at throwing a right to Ripley's jaw, but it was pitiful. He pulled away from it and a little smile came across his face. He kept me busy so I couldn't get the gun in firing position.

And then Urban appeared, flying through the air. He came from the bed and wrapped himself around Ripley's head. Ripley grunted. This time I moved fast for Urban's sake. The knife, once Ripley realized what was happening, could go right into Urb's neck or face.

I dropped the gun and grabbed Ripley's wrist. I bent his arm in an unnatural way and heard cracking. Ripley cried out and all the energy went out of his body. He dropped the knife. Then dropped to his knees.

"Get him off!" he squealed.

I kicked the knife behind me and picked up the .38. "Let him go, Urb."

"I'll kill him!" Urban said.

"Don't kill me!" Ripley said.

"Get off, Urban." I tapped his head with the gun butt.

He let go with a howl of protest.

"Please don't kill me," Ripley said. "You can have the money."

Urban smoothed his shirt. "Where is it?"

"In the closet."

My miniature cohort went over and came back with a nylon bag. He pawed through it. "It better all be here," he said.

Ripley said, "I spent a couple of thou."

"A couple of thou!" Urban said.

"Don't kill me. I got a wife."

"You should've thought of that before you ripped off Wincher!"

"Now listen, boys," I said. "Urban's got the money, what there is of it, to return to his boss. The boss won't be happy, but it will be unhappiness with you, Mr. Ripley."

"I'll take care of him," Urban said.

"We're going to let Mr. Ripley go."

"No!"

"Yes. And Mr. Ripley is going to get a four-hour head start. I'd advise you to get as far away from the city as you can. Call your wife and get her to meet you somewhere."

"You're really letting me go?" Ripley said.

"No!" Urban said.

"Yes," I said. "Start now."

. . .

WHILE RIPLEY GOT his stuff together, Urban yelled and cursed at me. I told him I would roll him down California Street if he didn't shut up.

Ripley left.

"Can I go now?" Urban said.

"I said we'd give him four hours."

"He's a thief!"

"That doesn't mean we lie to him. Haven't you heard of honor among thieves?"

"Hell no."

"You want a drink?"

"What've you got?"

I had two glasses and half a bottle of Jack in my room. We went back there. I poured. I gave a glass to Urban Rosetta and let him sit on the chair. His legs stuck out like a child's. I sat on the bed.

"You live in the city, Urb?"

"Yeah." He downed the booze in one crank and held out his glass for more. I poured him another shot.

"Ever kill anybody?" I said.

"No." One more down the pipe. He held out his glass again.

"Take it easy there, pal," I said.

"I can handle it," he said.

Before I poured I said, "You hit the stuff pretty regular?"

"What else is there to do?" he said. He wiggled his glass.

"Nurse it," I said, pouring. "Booze is a mocker, so they say."

"Who says?"

"I think it's the Bible," I said.

"Never read it," Urban Rosetta said.

"Never read the Bible?"

"It's not for me."

"Everybody's got to read it. It's the formative book of

Western Civ."

"I don't believe in that stuff." He took a sip of whisky.

"Doesn't matter," I said. "Ancient wisdom is good to know. Here." I went to the simple desk they had for me in the room and opened the left hand drawer and pulled out a burgundy-cover Gideon Bible. "There's a part in here called Proverbs. You ever heard of Proverbs?"

"Maybe."

I opened to the middle and found my way to Proverbs. "Listen up," I said. " 'Proverbs of Solomon the son of David, king of Israel. To know wisdom and instruction; to perceive the words of understanding. To receive the instruction of wisdom, justice, and judgment, and equity.' You hear that, Urb?"

"I got the part about judgment." He'd finished and held out his glass.

"One more," I said, and gave him a short one, which seemed fitting.

"Listen. 'A wise man will hear, and will increase learning; and a man of understanding shall attain unto wise counsels.' You don't want to be a splotch on the earth, do you? Just taking up space."

"I don't take up much space," he said, then snorted. "Can't believe I said that."

"You a pro torpedo?"

"What's that?"

"Gunman. Strong arm."

"Just for Wincher. I've known him a long time."

"You know people who kill people?" I said.

He shrugged. "You need somebody done?"

"No, somebody got done. It looks like a hired job to me."

"Who was it?"

"A young woman. She was on the news. She claimed a sexual liaison with Samuel Johnson."

"What's liaison?" he asked.

"A tryst."

"I don't know these words!"

"She said she had sex with Samuel Johnson."

"Who's that?"

"I guess you're not up on politics."

"I don't like politics. They're all liars."

"Not like us," I said.

He smiled. "Not like us." He raised his glass to me and drank.

After a pause, he said, "If there's anything I can do for you, just let me know. Urban Rosetta knows how to repay a debt."

"Where can I get hold of you, Urban Rosetta?"

"There's a bar, a lot of us go there."

"Us?"

"Vertically challenged, as they say. Man, that's a joke. I'm getting toasted. Place is called Johnny X. Ask anybody for me."

He finished his drink and slipped off the chair. He reeled a bit, then picked up the bag of money. It almost pulled him over.

Just before he left the room he said, "Thanks."

Nice little guy.

I WALKED HIM down to the lobby, where a few denizens sat watching the community TV. Local news. Just coming off the weather report.

Cold.

The male anchor with the dyed hair said something about "our lead story." He then handed it off to the field reporter, who barked into a microphone as yellow police tape fluttered behind him. I sometimes wonder if the news crews bring their own police tape and set up shots for themselves. Wouldn't surprise me.

Then came some stock shots of Samuel Johnson juxtaposed against what looked like T'Kia Wilson's driver's license photo.

Beside me in the lobby, two geezers—I'm being charitable here—were jawing about the news report. One was black, the other white.

"He got to her," the white guy said. "Shut her up good."

"You out your mind you think he had anything do with it," the black guy said. "He's too smart."

"Man does a lot worse things when a woman gets to him."

"Worse than killin'?"

"Marryin'," the white guy said, and the two of them laughed.

"Johnson's a good man," the black guy said.

"He's a politician, just like the rest of 'em, and he likes a little on the side. He just got caught is all," the white guy said.

"So he kills the lady?"

"She was gonna talk."

"You smokin' some of that reefer."

"I could use me some reefer."

They laughed again.

And so goes political discourse in a San Francisco hotel.

Things were going to be popping all over the Griffin campaign. Somebody was going to be ticked that the Sam Johnson business card wasn't found on the body. It was in just such an atmosphere that loose lips could leak inside dope.

I called Katarina Hogg. I asked if her offer of a place to stay was still open. She asked me if I was kidding and I said I wasn't and I'd explain later. She gave me her address.

KAT'S APARTMENT IN Pacific Heights was small but in exactly the right spot for a professional woman on the way up. The polished hardwood floor almost cried out for the shoes of deep-pocketed donors to be scuffing around sipping Martinis and chattering in superior tones about the things they chat-tered about. There was a white, L-shaped sofa facing view windows, and a single piece of artwork—a metallic abstract about four feet high—which was either a deep artistic reflec-tion on the plight of man, or something found in a junkyard after an earthquake.

Kat was dressed in jeans and a white pullover sweater. She could have been a college student on the way to class. The outfit brought out an earthier beauty in her, not like the styled, professional look that her position demanded.

After I dropped my duffel bag and thanked her, she said, "Let's have a look."

"A look?"

"Take your shirt off, big boy."

"You don't waste time, do you?" I said.

"Time is money," she said.

"Money is the root of all evil," I said.

"No," she said. "The *love* of money is the root of all evil. Don't misquote the Bible."

I winced as I went for the buttons of my shirt. Kat stepped close and started unbuttoning the shirt herself. She worked the buttons slowly.

She finished and slipped my shirt off. She gently turned me around, said, "It's time to change this."

I took out the bag of stuff the hospital had given me and handed it to her. She led me to the bathroom, which had a framed Erté print on the wall—a flapper from the 20s, leaning on a pillow, looking fetchingly off to the side.

Kat went about her work like a trauma nurse. She ripped off the bandages without remorse.

"Nice," she said.

"That's ambiguous." I said.

"We should take a picture and Instagram it. I'm glad this didn't get you in the spine."

She started to apply some of the tubed cream.

"Does that hurt?" she said.

"About the same as any other gunshot wound, more or less."

"You've had more?" she said.

"Just guessing."

Her hands were soothing on my back.

"Good thing you're like rock," she said. "Give your personal trainer my compliments."

"I just eat right," I said.

"Yeah? What?"

"Grubs, wild boar."

"You are so ..."

"Random?"

She finished with the topical and applied a pad and gauze and taped it all up.

I turned around and we faced each other, and for a moment, neither one of us moved.

"My shirt," I said.

"What about it?" she said.

"You better help me put it on."

She looked at my chest and at my mouth. "Shoot."

We went back to her living room. The lights of the city and the Golden Gate Bridge were popping in all their postcard splendor. Kat asked me if I'd like a drink and I said, "Anything but a Royal Romance."

She laughed and went into the kitchen. "No promises," she called back. "How about some wine?"

I sat on the sofa.

Kat came back in with a bottle of white wine and two glasses. She expertly uncorked the bottle and poured. She handed me a glass and sat on the sofa next to me, drawing her legs under her.

"To good health," she said.

"To order in the universe," I said.

We sipped. The wine was cold and crisp with notes of apricot and oak. Or maybe it was honey and toast. Or maybe I didn't care.

She said, "So explain to me why you tattooed Latin on your arm."

"It seemed like a good idea at the time."

"So you were drunk?"

"Just buzzed."

She laughed. "Really?"

"But of sound mind."

"So tell me what it means."

"Truth conquers all things."

She thought about it. "You believe that?"

"I did at the time and maybe still do."

"You're wavering?"

"You work in politics. You tell me."

"That's a low blow," she said.

"Is it?" I said.

"You don't have any right to judge me."

"I'm talking about the world you run in. Do you always tell the truth in your press releases?"

"You know how the game is played," she said.

"You feel okay about that?"

"It's not a question of feeling. It's a question of dealing with things as they are. There are good ends and bad ends and it's my job to try to make sure the good side wins."

"Who decides what is good?" I said.

"Sometimes it's obvious," she said.

"And other times?"

"It's not my job to think about the other times." She sipped more wine and shook her head a little.

I said, "Is it your job to think about the death of T'Kia Wilson?"

She looked at me evenly. "That's a terrible thing to say."

"I mean, how is the campaign going to spin it?"

"I hate that word," she said.

"That's your stock in trade, isn't it?" I said.

"You don't have to be nasty about it."

"Was I nasty?"

Kat ran a fingertip over the rim of her glass. "Most people think *spin* is just a fancy term for lying."

I nodded.

"But I don't deal in lies," she said. "I am an advocate for the facts, and facts are open to interpretation."

"Nicely said."

"You believe me?"

"That's open to interpretation," I said.

"I wish I could figure you out," she said.

"What fun would that be?"

A question that prompted Kat to get up and walk to the window. Her back to me, she looked out for a long time without saying a word. I watched her in her soft sweater, looking little against the massive darkening sky and jeweled lights outside. Not a master of the universe, because who really is?

I wanted to go to her. Give up and go. Forget what it might mean. Figure all that out later.

And then she turned around. She held her wine glass in both hands and looked into it. She did not move from the window.

"Mike, you don't have to go."

At that moment I didn't want to lie to her. So I didn't say anything.

"Damn," she said.

I got up and went to her, and when I got there she was shaking her head.

"I suppose I could be a little less obvious," she said.

"That would make me have to guess," I said.

"Like I'm doing now." She made kiss-me eyes that were very effective.

One of those long pauses they used to call pregnant followed.

Will power, Romeo.

"How about those Giants?" I said.

"If you weren't hurt, I'd hit you," she said. Now her eyes were cold steel.

"I'm glad you won't," I said. "I'm afraid of violence."

"Why do I have this sudden, horrible feeling that I'm making a great big mistake?"

"Because you are." At least that was an honest answer.

She said, "That only means you're a challenge. I can break you down."

"You want to fight?"

"Are you man enough?" she said.

"Gosh, you preacher's kids are tough." I said.

"And if you're not nice to me I will slap some Bible verses on you."

"A soft answer turneth away wrath," I said as I took one step forward, cursing silently.

"Answer not a fool according to his folly," she said.

My left arm wrapped around her neck. For a long moment our lips made like David and Bathsheba.

"You want to know me better?" I said.

"There is no going back now," she said.

"Then lend me your car."

She took a step back. "What?"

"With you in it, of course. I need to go looking for something. And I may need a partner."

"I like the sound of it," she said. "But why?"

"Somebody shot me," I said. "I take that personally."

"When do you want to go?"

"In the morning."

She kissed me again. "That means you're spending the night."

"Lead me not into temptation."

"Why don't you take a flying leap?" she said, and headed for the kitchen.

"That's not in the Bible," I said.

"It should have been," she said.

I WOKE UP on her sofa and for a minute forgot where I was. Then I thought I was in New York and I flashed back to when I was fourteen and in the West Side apartment of Zbysław Osage, the philosopher, a friend of my father's. It was a summer job and I was helping him do some research on the history of ontology in German thought. His apartment looked over Central Park and it was a rainy day and I remember thinking I should be outside playing football, football in the rain, but I was not built for football but for reading books.

I came to myself and remembered it was Kat's apartment and the day was starting to dawn. I smelled her. We'd held each other for a long time on the sofa last night before she went to bed and I went into a deep dream. In the dream, Harrison Ford was a priest in a hooded robe and he was out to get me.

I heard Kat in the kitchen. And smelled coffee. I flexed my shoulder and made a noise that was somewhere between a groan and a huff.

"Good morning," she said.

I sat up. All I had on was boxers. The blanket was warm over my legs.

She came to me.

"Not very modest this morning," she said, smiling, sat next me and put her hands on my chest, then wrapped them around my neck and kissed me.

It was a good way to start a morning. The kiss was long and full and when we finally parted I said, "Are you sure?"

"I'm sure," she said.

"What about me not telling you who I am?" I said.

"We can chance it."

"What about your work and my work?"

"You're full of questions," she said.

"Sometimes that's all I'm full of," I said.

"No questions right now. Coffee?"

"Oh yeah."

She went to the kitchen and came back with two large, earthenware mugs. She sat again and we drank the coffee black and it was like being in a ski lodge with her and I thought, *This is what a normal life is like, Romeo. This is what you could have if ...*

... if what? If I could take away every bad thing and the shadows that always pour out of me and cover anyone close?

When was the last time I'd kissed a woman like that, and I knew that I never had, there had always been a holding back and then a taking, and then it would be time to say goodbye and I would go and know that I'd left some of my shadow behind with her, and I hated that, but it didn't stop me from the taking.

But with Kat it was different. At least it was at that moment. But how long would that last before there would be another taking and another goodbye?

"I have to go into the office," she said.

"We never talk anymore," I said.

"Shut up. I can be back around eleven and take you where you want to go."

"I'd really like to go to New Zealand," I said.

"That'll have to wait." She stood. "Now drink your coffee and try not to mess up my place."

Five minutes later I heard the shower.

It was the sound of normal.

Something I hadn't known since the day my parents died.

I DID STAY with my aunt for a year. She and other well-meaning people who knew my parents tried to get me to go back to Yale.

But I wanted no part of Yale. Ever again.

When I turned eighteen I left my aunt a note and hit the road. Got in my old heap and drove south. When I was out of money I stopped. I was in Louisville.

Downtown.

Walking around.

I came to an odd marker. It was right there on the street. A permanent monument. It said this:

A Revelation

Merton had a sudden insight at this corner Mar. 18, 1958, that led him to redefine his monastic identity with greater involvement in social justice issues. He was "suddenly overwhelmed with the realization that I loved all these people...." He found them "walking around shining like stars."

Merton? Yeah, Thomas Merton, my mom had mentioned him once or twice.

What a sucker.

And I had my own revelation right there at that sign. My own idea about redefining my identity. And it didn't have anything to do with loving other people.

It had to do with giving other people what they deserved.

It would start with my body and end with my mind.

I found a gym that taught boxing and martial arts. The guy who ran it was Demetrius Boland, out of Jersey. I knew how to talk to guys from Jersey. So he gave me a job cleaning up, with a small room to stay in.

In return, he taught me how to fight.

And eat.

And push weights.

In a year and a half I was an absolutely new person, made of cement, with unfinished business in New Haven.

KAT KISSED ME and then left for the office, as if we were in an upside-down episode of *Leave It to Beaver*.

I called Ira.

"What's going on?" he said.

"I'm living with a woman," I said.

Silence.

"Temporarily," I said.

"Katarina Hogg?"

"The very same," I said. "She's giving me a bed."

"Dear God."

"On her sofa," I said.

"Why am I not comforted?" Ira said. "By the way, the building where you found the Wilson girl has strange ownership. Two shell corporations involved. That's not uncommon, and neither one lists officers or directors. But they have to have an agent for service of process, and they both have the same one. A lawyer named Gail Goodman. Office in Sausalito."

"Maybe I should pay her a visit," I said.

"Hold on there, Lightning. Let me do some more digging before you go blustering into somebody's office."

"I glide, Ira. I never bluster."

A very audible sigh glided into my ear.

. . .

THAT AFTERNOON KAT drove us over to Walnut Creek.

She talked about her childhood and strict upbringing and how sneaking a listen to The Backstreet Boys was her first act of rebellion. She asked me about my first act of rebellion.

"You'll laugh," I said.

"No I won't," she said.

"I stayed up all night, under the covers with a flashlight, reading *The Nature and Destiny of Man*."

She didn't laugh. "How old were you?"

"Seven," I said.

"Seven? And you were reading, what was it again?"

"*The Nature and Destiny of Man* by Reinhold Niebuhr."

"It doesn't sound like a kid's book."

"Depends on the kid."

"And you rebelled by reading a forbidden book?" she asked.

"No, by staying up all night. My mom wanted me to get eight hours."

She said, "I think you must have some serious brain power going on."

"Brain power is overrated," I said.

We changed the subject and drove on, and when we got to the Walnut Creek neighborhood I made a change. I gave her the address and went into the back of her car, where I could lie down, with instructions to drive by slowly once. She could be a woman out looking for houses on the market.

As she drove by the house, I asked her what she saw.

"Looks like a nice house. Neat. A couple of cars in the driveway."

"What kind?"

"A nice black one, looks like a Caddy. The other one is an SUV. Mercedes. There's a black pickup at the curb."

"Any people around?"

"I don't see any."

I popped up enough to look out the window. It was as she

described.

"Keep going," I said. "Around the block. Go back around to the beginning of the street."

She did. I had her pull over just past the corner. From here we could see the house. It was halfway down on the left. Of the two cars in the driveway, the black Caddy was closest to us.

It was the Caddy that had my interest now, more pieces floating around in my head crying out for connection, but they didn't line up.

"Now for some instructions," I said.

"Tell me, captain."

"We watch. We surveil. You into surveillance?"

"Totally."

"You know the secret of surveillance?"

"Do tell."

"Not to be caught surveilling."

"Makes sense."

"So we're going to have to do something really daring. Are you ready to get daring?"

"Let's."

"When we see people walking by, we have to kiss each other."

"I like this surveillance stuff."

"That way people will think we're a couple of crazy kids in love. Think you can handle that?"

"I'll give it my best shot. Let's rehearse."

We did. It was a good rehearsal. In fact, it was ready for opening night.

We watched for an hour and went into our dance a couple of times. I started hoping more people would walk by.

In between we talked, and I found in Kat a mind that was curious about my world, which is a world of ideas. She wanted to know what made me tick, and why I wouldn't tell her too much about my past.

I told her one step at a time.

Then someone came out of the house. It was a man, dressed like a guy going to the grocery store. Medium height, dark hair. He walked around to the back of the Caddy and bent over. He put his hand on the rear license plate. He appeared to jiggle the plate. He popped the trunk and took something out. It was a tool of some kind. He appeared to be tightening the rear license plate.

I said, "Uh-huh."

"What?" Kat said.

"The car that shot me, it had a bum plate."

Somebody else came out. It was the kid with the stringy hair, one of the two who hit me when I first arrived. His right hand had what looked like a splint on his finger. He said something to the man and they talked and the vibe was father and son.

The kid went back inside and the man got into the Cad.

"What do we do now?" Kat said.

"Can you follow him?"

"Kiss me."

I kissed her.

"I can do anything," she said. The car pulled out of the driveway and headed away from us.

"Wait a second," I said. "Give him a lead."

"Bonnie and Clyde," she said.

"Nick and Nora Charles," I said.

"Who are they?"

"I'll tell you later, over martinis."

"I like them already."

"Go."

I coached her on distance and we followed the Caddy down two main drags. A couple of miles went by and then he pulled into the parking lot of a Lowe's. He took a space, got out, headed for the store.

I had Kat park a few spaces away.

"Think you can get a picture of this guy without him knowing it?"

"I'm so good with that."

"You need to be. He can't have any idea."

"I can try."

"Do, or do not. There is no try."

"Okay. Do."

"Go and make me proud," I said.

She headed into the store. I called Ira.

"Mike, how are you?"

"Like a one winged dove," I said. "I need you to run a plate."

"You never just call me anymore."

I ignored him and gave him the plate number.

"When do you need it?" he said.

"A week ago."

"That'll take me a little longer. Where are you?"

"I'm out in the field. I'm with her."

He said, "Is this going to interfere with your work?"

"It's making the work tolerable," I said.

"Can it be I sense a note of humanity in your voice?"

"I wouldn't jump to any conclusions. Be quick about your business."

"Don't be so abrupt."

I cut the call.

Waited.

Ten minutes. Kat came out, smiling.

"I got it," she said. "I'm good."

"I had no doubt. Send it to me." I gave her my phone number.

"This is fun," she said. "Going on Facebook?"

"Sure."

"Now what?"

"We go back to the city."

"It's such a nice day," she said.

"I hate to ruin it," I said.

She smiled at first, then saw I was serious.

"What?" she said.

"Tell me what you know about T'Kia Wilson."

Kat blinked a couple of times. I could almost hear the eyelids clack.

"I don't know that much about her," she said.

"You're right in the middle of the campaign," I said. "She was big news, and now even bigger in death."

"Just what are you suggesting?"

"She was a nuclear weapon."

"Meaning?"

"To take out Samuel Johnson once and for all."

"He got caught," Kat said. "The public has a right to know."

"Or the whole thing was manufactured."

"We have the evidence. Her lawyer, Sylvia Alton, has it."

"Evidence can be manufactured, too," I said.

"He was in Chicago the same time T'Kia was. There are receipts."

"What was T'Kia Wilson doing in Chicago?"

"I don't know! Why are you doing this, Mike?"

"Doing what?"

"Cross-examining me. I don't like it."

"Somebody shot me. Somebody tried to kill me or Leeza Edgar. Somebody killed T'Kia Wilson. I want to know the connections."

"What do you expect me to do about it?"

"Tell me the truth."

"You ... I don't believe ..."

"What's wrong with the truth?" I said.

Her eyes flamed. "Have you been truthful with me?"

Bam.

"Well?" she said.

"I haven't told you everything about myself," I said.

"Start," she said.

"Trade," I said.

"Maybe."

I said, "I work for a lawyer. He hired me to find out about T'Kia Wilson."

Kat's jaw muscles twitched. I could sense the words forming, the various names she wanted to pin on me.

Finally, she said, "Get out."

"You don't want to know the truth about T'Kia, do you?"

"Get out!"

"What if T'Kia was a hit job?"

I tried to read her eyes, looking for nystagmus, an involuntary twitching that happens with those who have something to hide. All she did was blink.

"Who would do that?" she said.

"You don't have any ideas?"

She shook her head.

"Would Jay J. Parsons know?" I said.

"You're not ... There's no way."

"Can you arrange a meeting?" I said.

"After all this? After you freaking lied to me?"

"What couple doesn't have its squabbles?"

"Squabble!" She clenched her face like she was trying to keep her head from exploding. "I can't believe I was so stupid."

"You're not," I said. I took her hand. She left it for a moment then pulled it away.

She looked at her hands and spoke softly. "You were going to just lie and then run out."

"I was," I said. "I don't want to now."

She looked at me, confusion and hurt and anger on her face.

"Set up the meeting with Jay J," I said. "I'll lay it all out for both of you."

"He fired you," she said. "He doesn't want to see you."

"Give him a reason. Tell him I came to see you, which I did, and that I can provide him some information on the T'Kia Wilson killing, which I can. That should be enough."

"What do you know about the killing?"

"I'll talk that over at the meeting."

"You don't have anything at all, do you?"

"I might have a card up my sleeve," I said.

"Why should I believe anything you say?"

"Dammit, because I'm charming," I said.

Her mouth fought a smile then gave in to a grimace.

"I won't lie to you again," I said.

"Who is the lawyer you work for?" she said.

"I can't tell you," I said.

"Ha!"

"It's confidential," I said. "You should know that."

"Does he work for the Johnson campaign?"

"Let me put it this way. The lawyer I work for is interested in only one thing, the truth."

She said, "I find it really ironic that a guy with a truth tattoo lied to me."

"I'll change it," I said. "To a skull with *Born to Lose* underneath."

"Just keep it," she said. "Maybe it'll sink in."

OUR LAST STOP was Leeza Edgar's apartment building. I didn't expect she'd be there. She'd been grilled by the Dogs and then shot at—at least, she was there when the shots were fired.

There was no answer when I buzzed.

So I buzzed the next-door apartment.

A buzzy voice, a woman's, came through the speaker.

"Yeah?"

"I'm trying to get hold of Leeza Edgar," I said.

"Who?"

"Leeza Edgar."

"Wrong apartment."

"I mean next door."

"What?"

"In 2C."

"She's gone."

"Can you tell me where?"

Click.

I went back to Kat's car. "I think I'll watch the place for a while," I said. "Then I'll come and get my stuff."

"You don't need to," she said. "Yet."

As she drove away I thought about that *yet*. Three letters. But on them history has changed, wars have been started, and lovers have been thrown together and pulled apart. It has dread or hope ahead of it, and sometimes you just don't know which it will turn out to be.

But I had a feeling about *yet* now, and it wasn't good.

After an hour and half sitting at the bus stop bench on the corner, and seeing no one who looked like Leeza Edgar, even in a heavy disguise, I called it quits. The wind was starting to change from playful biting to insistent gnawing.

But I wasn't about to let this city chew me up.

AROUND EIGHT I went to the place called Johnny X. It was in the Tenderloin. It had a nondescript black door and a simple red X on it. I pushed inside to find the medium lights of a drinking establishment. No mood here. Just a set up for the crushing of fast drinks. It could have been any bar along a back street except for one item. A small pool table close to the ground.

Here a couple of Urban's cohorts played a game. One of the two was considerably shorter than his opponent, who was short to begin with. So he used a small step for elevation before the shot.

"You sure you're in the right place?"

She was about three feet tall, blonde, wearing a leather jacket, and holding a Corona.

"Do you serve my kind in here?" I said.

"No discrimination, big boy," she said. "Where you from?"

She cast a glance at my attire, which was a Hawaiian shirt with pineapples on it under a brown jacket and over blue jeans.

"I'm here on a little business," I said. When she squinted I said, "Sorry. Just business."

She softened. "Let's dance," she said.

"Do you know Urban Rosetta?"

"Come on." She reached out to me.

"Another time," I said.

She slapped her hip with the hand I'd refused. "What do you want with Urb?"

"I'm a friend."

"You don't look like a friend."

"What do I look like?"

"Big trouble."

I said, "Inside I'm small and peaceful."

"You try anything in here you'll get hurt."

I looked around the place. "Tough crowd, huh?"

"Don't underestimate the under fours," she said.

"My name's Mike."

"Rose."

"Nice to meet you, Rose. Know where I can find him?"

"Order a drink," she said.

I resisted the urge to say, *You mean at the mini-bar?* and went over and ordered a Coke.

I took the Coke and went to the pool table. The guy who

used the step hit a nice combination. He gave me a hard look.

"You shoot a good stick," I said.

"How much?" he said.

"How much what?" I said.

"Friendly game."

"I don't shoot with pool hustlers," I said. I meant it as a joke, but the little guy got off his step and faced me, meaning my thigh. "You calling me a hustler?" he said.

"You mean you're not hustling me?"

"You want to step outside?"

I noticed his opponent and some of the others in the bar looking at me. Was I really being challenged to a fight?

I put my hands up in surrender. "No way, man."

"Then back off," he said.

"*You* back off, Max." It was Urban.

Max turned on Urban, holding his miniature pool cue like a weapon. "You want a piece of this?"

Rose stepped between them. "Cut it out, you dopes!"

Urban said, "Mike, come on."

"Don't be a stranger," Rose said.

Urban led me past the bar top and through a back door. In another room was a round table with guys—a mix of big and little—playing poker. One of the little ones smoked a pipe.

They gave us a passing glance and continued playing.

Urb said, "What are you doing here?"

"I need some information, and you were the only one I could think of who could give it to me."

He nodded. "You want a drink?"

"Not tonight."

"Spill."

I took out my phone and showed him the picture of the man from Walnut Creek.

Urban gave it a long look, shook his head. "Who is he?"

"I think he's a mechanic," I said.

"A hit man?"

I nodded.

"He looks normal," Urban said.

"That's the best look, isn't it? Live a life of ease and comfort, nice family man, do a little shooting on the side."

"He the one who got you?"

"Could be. He has a kid, and his kid and a buddy of his attacked me when I first got here to Frisco."

"We don't like it when outsiders say Frisco."

I closed my eyes. "The guy you work for, think he'd know?"

"Might. But who's gonna ask him?"

"Me."

"No way. Can't be done."

"Anything can be done."

"Not that."

Somebody from the poker table said, "You playing or not, Rosetta?"

"Deal me out," Urb said.

"Then shut up," the guy said.

"Bite me," Urb said. He took me through another door, and we were outside.

"You don't know Wincher," Urb said. "He's bad."

"That's why I want to see him."

"I told you—"

"I'll make him an offer."

"What kind of offer you got he'd want?"

"Guy like that always wants something."

"Money."

"Other than money."

"What else is there?"

"Information," I said.

"You got something like that?"

"Could very well be," I said.

"Aw, no—"

"Urb, do me this and we'll be square."

"Square? You mean about Ripley?"

"That's right."

"Aw, man. I don't know."

"Just get me in," I said. "What'll you have to drink?"

WE WENT BACK to the bar and I ordered Urban a shot.

I said, "Make the call."

"You better have something worth listening to."

"Urb, have I ever lied to you?"

"You banged me into a wall!"

"But I did not lie. That's the main thing."

He sighed. "Let me make a call. I can't promise anything. I have to talk to a guy who can talk to a guy."

"Sounds like a federal government website."

He blinked. "Wait here."

I waited, leaning on the bar. Rose came over.

"What are you two into?" she said.

"We're trying to bring back vaudeville," I said.

"What's that?"

"Specialized stage acts. Song and dance, sketches."

She scrunched her face. "You're pulling my leg."

"I bet it's a nice leg."

Smiling, she kicked one of her legs out. "Thanks. Let me see your arm."

"Which one?"

"The one with the tat."

I held out my left so she could read it. "What's it mean?"

"Truth conquers all things."

"Cool. Does it?"

It seemed every time I got asked that question my view would change. I was changing, so how could it be the same?

"I think you have to believe it does," I said. "Because if you don't, why go on?"

Rose thought about it. I like that. I like when people think about it.

"I think lies usually win," she said. "Look at politics."

I almost snorted. "You're insightful, Rose. But what I'm talking about is you, the individual, all of us, looking around for some reason to live. If there's no truth out there, if we just make stuff up, there's really no point."

"Yeah, but maybe there isn't. Maybe there isn't real truth."

"It's why we've got to keep looking. The looking is part of it. It's a reason to get up in the morning."

"You're a strange guy," she said.

"So I've been told."

"I like you."

"I like you too, Rose. Can I buy you another beer?"

"Beer overcomes all things, too," she said, and laughed.

I ordered her a Corona and we talked for a few more minutes. She was from Hollywood and her parents had been in the movies. There'd been a Chevy Chase movie about Munchkins and they'd had good roles, and Rose was a baby in a scene that got cut. She'd come to San Francisco to find her own way of life.

Urban came back.

"You're in luck," he said.

"Come back and see me sometime," Rose said.

I PAID FOR a cab. Urban gave the driver an address on Washington Street. It was red-brick office building with an old-fashioned arch over the front door. A definite 1930s vibe.

Inside was a security console with a very large man in a blue coat behind it.

"Help you?" he said.

Urban said, "We have an appointment with Mr. Wincher."

"May I have your names?"

"Urban Rosetta and guest."

"Ah. One moment, please." He picked up a handset and pressed a button, put it to his ear. "A Mr. Rosetta and guest are here to see Mr. Wincher. Uh-huh. All right."

He put the handset down. "Please step over to the metal detector."

He stood up and was even bigger than I thought. He came around his station and over to the detector. He positioned himself on the other side. "If you will please remove the contents of your pockets. Watches, bracelets."

Urb put change and a wallet in a plastic bowl. I tossed my wallet and some loose change in another.

Urb went through first and the security gate went nuts. The big guy motioned for Urban to approach him.

"I don't understand," Urban said.

"This won't take a second," the big man said, and he had to lean way over to pat down Urban Rosetta. But he came back up with the .38 that was in the back of Urb's pants.

He looked at Urban with stark disapproval.

"I forgot I had it!" Urban said.

"This is an oversight on your part. I will have to report it."

"Come on, man."

"One moment, please." He motioned for me to walk through and I did without a hitch. Then he took the gun and walked back to his console and made another call.

He came back to us. "Mr. Wincher will see you. I will hold your piece for you. You want the third floor, to the right. All the way down."

We got on the elevator. It was made of black iron. We could watch the pulleys and gears.

On the third floor we walked to the end of the corridor. Double doors made of rose-colored wood were the end of the line. Urban knocked.

A door opened and a man who looked like a German tank answered. He had short blond hair and blue eyes and was wide at the shoulders He led us into a reception area. There was a fish tank in one corner, lit up with blue and pink lights. A big flat fish swam contentedly around. Some littler fish gave way to the big fish.

"One moment," he said, and went through an inner door.

I watched the fish.

Urban shuffled around, mumbling.

"Don't be so nervous," I said.

"You're the one should be nervous," he said.

The German tank came back and said we could come in.

CEDRIC WINCHER SAT behind a nice-sized desk in an office with low lighting. He had a round head with big round eyes and fleshy lips. His hair was curly and brown with a little salt in it. He was just south of sixty, I guessed. He could have used a few more salads in his diet.

He wore a black silk shirt opened wide at the collar. Sprigs of white chest hair wove around a thick, gold-chain necklace. He held an e-cigarette in the fingers of his right hand.

"So you are the man I've been hearing so much about," Wincher said. "Let me have a look at you."

He motioned at me with the e-cigarette, like he wanted me to turn around. I just stared at him.

"You're a big fellow," he said. "Who can handle himself. And we all know there are many situations that need to be handled."

"Like this one," I said.

"Sure," Wincher said. "Would you like a drink?"

"No, thanks."

"Mind if I?"

I shook my head.

"Val, make me a gimlet, please."

The German tank went to a mobile bar in the corner and started to work.

"You know, I love a good gimlet," Wincher said. "It's a Hemingway drink. You read those safari stories and they all drink gimlets."

So he was going to be a talker. And not because he liked to hear himself, though that was pretty clear. It was how he was establishing control. I'd let him. But only for as long as I could stand it.

The man named Val came over to the table with the drink and handed it to Wincher.

"You have been granted a great privilege," Wincher said, then drank. "Ah, that's nice."

"Thanks for seeing me," I said.

"Urban here has proven valuable to me, and that's what got you in here. I believe people should have to prove themselves before I trust them. Do you think that's a good policy Mr. ... what was it again?"

"Romeo."

"Like the play."

Oh, he was sharp.

"I never liked Shakespeare," Wincher said. "Had to read *Othello* in high school. Black guy kills a white chick. Some plot. I mean, what do you call that?"

"Iambic pentameter," I said.

"Eh?"

"Ten syllables per line."

"Clever," Wincher said, and sucked some vapor. "I'm listening."

"Thought we might trade some information," I said.

Wincher motioned for me to continue.

"I'm trying to identify someone," I said.

"A mechanic, Mr. Rosetta said."

I nodded.

"Why would I know such things?" Wincher said.

I said, "Are we really going to do this?"

"Mike!" Urb said in a loud whisper.

Wincher raised his hand. "It's all right. I was just wondering, Mr. Romeo, if you're a good fighter. You look like it, but looks are one thing, doing it another."

"I don't like to fight," I said.

"But you do if you have to, yes?"

"I prefer good conversation."

"Do you think you can fight Val over there?"

I craned around to look at Val. He smiled at me.

"I don't want to fight your man," I said. "That's not why I'm here."

"And Mike has a bad wing," Urban said.

"Mr. Rosetta," Wincher said, "I would like you to stay out of this particular discussion. Is that understood?"

Urban looked at his boots.

"What do you say, Mr. Romeo?"

"No thanks."

"Are you afraid?"

"Sure," I said.

"I don't think you are," Wincher said. "I'd like you to show Val what you're made of."

"What good is all this?" I said.

"You came here, I understand, to offer me something. In return, I am supposed to help you if I can."

"Yes."

"But I don't think you have anything that would interest me. Nor do I think I can trust you. But if you would consent to give Val a tangle, I might change my mind."

Wincher took a sip of his drink and looked at me.

I said, "We'll be going now."

I turned.

Val moved in front of the door.

"Let's see what you can do," Wincher said.

I sighed. "Does he have any metal on him?"

"Val, do you have any weaponry on you?"

Val shook his head.

"All right," I said like a defeated man, and took a couple of steps to the side, toward the mobile bar.

Val smiled and started to take off his coat. When it was halfway down I grabbed the neck of a bottle of Gordon's Dry Gin. Val's arms were still in his coat when I backhanded his face with the bottle. It smashed against his left temple. Glass shattered and gin splashed.

Val did not go down. But he reeled.

I snagged a bottle of Jameson and got him in the back of the head—that spot where all the wiring gets funneled into the brain.

Another shattering, and down he went.

"Mike!"

I turned and saw Urban attached to Wincher's head like a squid. Wincher's right hand held a gun. All that was keeping Wincher from firing was Urb's left foot, jamming Wincher's arm.

I grabbed the gun barrel and twisted against his thumb. The gun came free. I opened a desk drawer, put Wincher's hand in it and slammed it closed with my knee.

Wincher howled like a pig in a Chinese butcher shop. I kneed the drawer again and felt the crunch of bone.

"Get off him, Urb," I said.

My little protector let go and landed butt-first on the desk.

I took a handful of Wincher's curls and slammed his face into the wood. He came back up blood-smeared. Val was still down on the floor in a sea of booze.

"Watch him," I said to Urb. "If he starts to move, hit him with the Stoli."

I kept my leg against the drawer and said, "I'm only going to give you one chance. If I don't like your answer, you're going to end up like your friend there. Is that clear?"

His eyes were shut. He snuffed. A tiny red bubble squeezed out of his right nostril and popped.

I took out my phone and thumbed to the photo. I put it on the desk in front of Wincher. "Look at it."

He kept his eyes closed. I took hold of his hair and again and said, "You want to talk to your desk again?"

He opened his eyes. I bent his head down. "You tell me who that is, or I mix a gimlet with your eyeball."

"Wait," he snuffled. "Wait ... what if I don't ... know?"

"Urb, bring me the Stoli."

"Wait! Yeah, okay, his name's Whitehead. He's a pro. Please!"

"Now I want you to take another look, because I believe you gave me the wrong name."

"No—"

"I've killed eighteen men, all better than you. I've killed them up close, like this, so I can look in their eyes. I like looking in their eyes. If I were to leave here and find out you gave me a bogus name, then I'd have to wait around for you and—"

I picked up a picture frame from his desk. A woman and a teenager, obviously his wife and daughter.

"And them," I said.

"Please," Wincher said.

I put the frame face down on the desk, slid off the backing, took out the photo. I folded it once and put it in my back pocket.

"For future reference," I said. "Name."

"It ... okay, his name's Orrie Smoltz. He can't know I told you."

Smoltz. Now wasn't that something? Same name as one of the guys who attacked me that first night in the city.

"I do believe that's the right answer, Cedric," I said.

"Let me go, please. I've got no feeling in my hand!"

"Just a couple more things," I said. "I want you to listen to me, Cedric, because your life depends on it. Are you listening? Good. When I go from this place you are going start thinking how you can find me and kill me, but I cannot be found. But you can. I can find anybody. I can get to anybody."

This much I believe to be true.

"And if I ever even have a feeling, a twinge in my loins, that you are sending someone to find me, I'm going to find you and look into your eyes, Cedric. Do you understand what I'm saying to you?"

He gave one tired, defeated nod. But I wasn't ready to stop.

"Now, I know you, Cedric. Even with this warning, which I give you in good faith, more good faith than you have showed anyone in your life, you're going to think, no, I can get away with it. He'll never find me. The last man who thought that died screaming in a fire, the fire that consumed his body and his entire family."

Wincher just dropped his chin onto his chest.

"And by the way, this goes for my friend here. If he gets a twinge in his loins, I am going to look you in the eye, and in the eyes of your precious wife and daughter."

That's when Wincher let out one, sad, defeated whimper. I almost felt bad for what I was about to do.

"I have to put you to sleep now, Cedric."

"No ..."

"When you wake up, you'll have a terrible headache. You'll probably vomit. You should go see a doctor."

"Please ..."

"And when you dream, dream of me."

I took hold of Wincher's hair once more. He cried one last

time and then I made an imprint on the desk with Cedric
Wincher's face.

He was out.

"Damn," Urban said.

"Let's go," I said.

In the lobby I gave the security guard a wave.

OUTSIDE, IN THE brisk night, I walked fast. Urb had to
hurry to keep up with me.

"Is it true?" he said.

I didn't say anything. If I stopped moving I was going to eat
Urban Rosetta like the animal I was. I used to call this part of
me Achilles, as in crazy anger unleashed. But that was being
too kind.

"You really kill eighteen men?" Urb said.

I kept walking.

"Did you really burn a family alive?"

"I may have puffed my resume a bit," I said.

"You are one sick dude," he said.

We were three blocks away now, heading down a steep
Frisco street.

"Quit walking so fast!" Urban said from behind.

I walked faster.

"I'm okay with sick!" Urb said. "Come on, slow down!"

"INTERESTING DECOR," I said.

We were in Urban Rosetta's studio apartment on Taylor
Street. It was on the third floor of a community development
building across from a discount parking lot. The walls were
pale green. On one wall were three nudes, cut or torn from
magazines, taped up. On the facing wall was a one-foot
crucifix.

"I'm dead," Urban said.

"You saved my life," I said.

"What good will *that* do me?" He grabbed a pair of boxer shorts off a chair and threw them across the room. They landed under the crucifix.

Urb flopped in the chair, arms folded.

"In ancient China," I said, "when one man saved another man's life, he became responsible for that man forever."

"Really?"

"No. I actually think that was from an episode of *Kung Fu*, an old TV show. But still."

"You're no help."

"Maybe I am. You have anything holding you here?"

"Not anymore," he said. "I thought I might get ahead, but now that's shot."

"Why don't you come down to L.A.?"

"And do what?"

"Whatever you do here, only legally. I don't think you're a very good thug."

"Thanks again."

"But you're a good man," I said.

He looked shocked. "I am?"

"What a guy does in a crisis, without time to think, that's what tells you the kind of man he is."

Urb got quiet then. He slid off his chair and went to the window, looked out. His shoulders shook a little. I let him be.

When he turned back around he was wiping his nose with the back of his sleeve.

"Nobody ever told me that before," he said.

"I'm glad to be the first," I said. "Mind if I crash here tonight?"

"Oh yeah," Urb said.

"I've got some thinking to do," I said.

· · ·

IN THE MORNING I called Kat.

"What happened to you last night?" she said.

"I was out with a friend," I said. "I slept at his place."

"You have a friend?"

Urb was at his kitchenette stove, firing up the coffee.

"Is that so hard to believe?" I said.

"I mean here in the city."

"San Francisco has its charms," I said. "I've met some very nice people."

"Present company included?" she said.

"It's been a ride," I said.

"That is one of the most ambiguous answers I've ever heard."

"Like the man said, Give me ambiguity or give me something else."

Pause.

"Are you coming back here?" she said.

"You have my stuff."

"I've never heard such romantic talk," she said.

"I've got some things to do," I said. "But you are definitely going to see me again."

"Snap it up," she said.

I SAID GOODBYE to Urban Rosetta. When his hand disappeared in mine, and we shook, I thought about the poet John Donne again.

For at least this one moment I wasn't an island.

But as a piece of land, I was pretty raw. So I walked to an old fashioned barber shop on Mission and got a haircut and a shave and my cheeks slapped with Lilac Vegetal.

Then I hoofed over to a rental car place on O'Farrell and sat in the office for an hour while they prepped me a gray Corolla. The color matched my mood. My shoulder still hurt and I'd gotten a little guy into a lot of trouble, and a woman I had no business getting involved with was wrapping herself around my brain.

And in the middle of it all a dead girl who was the grand-daughter of a lovely woman, another random tragedy in the midst of this vale of tears.

Hobbes wrote that life was nasty, brutish, and short.

What a great brochure for life.

It also applies to rental cars. Inside the Corolla it smelled like air freshener trying to cover for an open can of Vienna wieners, and losing.

That put me in exactly the right mood for kidnapping.

Which is why I stopped at a True Value and picked up a roll of all-climate duct tape before heading over to Walnut Creek.

I PICKED UP on the Smoltz kid, Neil, a little after noon. He drove a black pickup, a nice one. Easy to follow.

Which I did. To Fuddruckers, then to somebody's house for a couple of hours. Back to his own house and then to a park where he met a girl and had a smoke.

Long and dull is the life of a real private investigator. I knew that because of Joey Feint. Feint worked in West Haven, Connecticut. Shortly after I came back to New Haven from my stint in Louisville, I saw Joey's name in a news story about a criminal case. Joey Feint was the investigator. The lawyer was a man my dad had known, Art Trackman. He'd been a student of my dad's.

So I went to see Joey Feint in his cramped little office. Joey himself could've been described as cramped and little. He wasn't much over five-foot-six, pudgy, with squinty eyes and round eyeglasses. No hair on his head but he had a hat rack full of hats by his door.

"Don't hurt me," he said the moment I walked through the door. "I'll get you the money."

I told him I wasn't the guy he was afraid of.

"That's a relief," he said. "For a moment there I thought I was going to have to shoot. What can I do for you?"

I told him who I was. He listened to the whole story with sadness mapped across his face. "I knew your dad," he said. "I met him when I was working for Art Trackman. What a lovely man. God, I'm sorry."

I told him there was something about the killings that still gnawed at me. In my gut, I felt it wasn't random. Maybe I was nuts, but I told him I wanted to hire him to find out as much as he could about the shooter, Benjamin Weeden Blackpoole, and dig into the whole case again. I also told him I had no money.

"What would you think about working for me?" he asked.

And that's how I became an apprentice to Joey Feint, and learned some of the finer points of PI work.

Like digging into county files that hadn't been digitized yet.

I read police reports, autopsy reports on all the victims, including four pages on my own parents. Reading about their condition was like living through the whole nightmare again, me being the one taking the bullets.

But it was in the report on Blackpoole that I found something the newspapers ignored. Because they didn't know what it meant.

I knew.

Among the things found in Blackpoole's apartment were an overabundance of illegally obtained antidepressants, several weapons, and an odd assortment of books and papers, the most curious of which was a little pamphlet about the Chinese philosopher Yang Chu.

The Yang Chu school had its high point in the fourth century BC, during what's called the Hundred Schools of

Thought period. The most famous saying of the Yang school was that if by plucking one hair of his head he could save all of mankind, the true Yang would not do it. Why? Because there is no God, no afterlife, and that sentimental nonsense is for fools. The wicked seem to prosper, so being wicked is good if it brings you pleasure.

I knew all this because of something that happened with my father. As a young philosophy student at Yale in the 1960s, he was going through the stacks in the library one day when he found a bound monograph on Yang Chu that had been misfiled. He read it, finding it of historical interest, then gave it to a librarian for proper shelving.

That was the last he saw of it until 1993. Then it was presented to him, word for word, in a student essay. Just to make sure, my father went to the library to try to find the monograph again. It was no longer there.

But it was in my father's photographic memory.

He confronted the student, who denied everything.

My father recommended the student's expulsion.

The student fought back, demanded an administrative hearing, where he accused my father of persecuting him. This student had a lawyer threaten to sue the university.

Because my father could not produce the monograph, the board was all set to let the student remain.

Then a friend of my father's who taught at the University of Missouri found another copy of the monograph and FedExed it to my dad.

My father presented it to the disciplinary board, along with the student paper, and that was that.

The student, Thurber McDaniels, was kicked out of Yale for good.

I started following McDaniels. Practiced the Joey Feint method of surveillance—pee beforehand, wear gray shirts, stay on the other side of the street, and wear the Joey Feint specially designed glasses with tiny side view mirrors on the inside.

And record the patterns.

McDaniels worked at a print shop near the Yale campus. He walked there most days. Took a lunch break, usually alone, but on consecutive Tuesdays he had a companion at Rusty's Subs. A kid around twenty, with frizzy red hair and wire-rim glasses. He looked like an Irish Bolshevik, talking and listening intensely to the more laid-back, and much older, Thurber McDaniels.

Irish guy became my second target of interest.

He lived in a small apartment near the campus.

It was Joey Feint who taught me the pizza box delivery trick, so that's what I did. Brought a boxed pizza to the door, knocked, Irish asked who it was, I said the pizza he ordered, and he said he didn't order, and I held up a ticket to the peephole.

Irish opened the door. I handed him the ticket. He looked at it.

"That's my number," he said, "but I didn't order this."

"Maybe a friend did," I said. "Prank. It happens."

He shook his head.

All this time I'm taking pictures of his apartment with a timed digital camera, the eye of which was embedded in a Joey Feint wristwatch he'd collected, he insisted, from one of Whitey Bulger's crew down in Boston.

"Well, it's just going to the trash," I said. "You want it?"

"No," he said, and slammed the door.

When I blew up the pictures the first thing I looked at was the bookshelf. It was one made up of cinderblocks and planks. Enlarging the photos made it easy to read most of the titles.

The boy was quite a military fan.

There were books on tactics, weapons, self-defense. A lot of World War II books, and a copy of *Mein Kampf*.

And right next to it a volume entitled *Yin and Yangism: On Self-Interest and Overcoming*.

Now, Joey Feint always told me to make sure the picture was complete before taking any action. The temptation, he would say, is always to move too fast.

I should have waited.

The next night I delivered a pizza to Thurber McDaniels.

When he got around to opening the door to look at the ticket, I stepped inside and closed the door for him.

"Hey!" he said.

McDaniels was forty or so. His springy black hair was balding fast on top, giving him the start of that Larry Fine look. He was half a foot shorter than I.

"Sit down," I said.

"You can't come in here," he said.

"I'm already in."

He looked me up and down and must have thought I was a leg-breaker.

"You're making a mistake," he said.

The apartment was neat. One could say obsessively so. Nothing too colorful. The place seemed like a drab but spotless piece of cloth.

"You were around for the shootings at Yale a couple of years ago," I said.

He fanned his hands outward. "I live here. So what?"

"You knew Benjamin Blackpoole," I said.

It was the pause that did it. And the narrowing of eyes that he tried not to narrow.

"Who are you?" he said.

"So you did know him," I said.

"Lots of people did. The cops even questioned me."

I shook my head. "The police never talked to you. I've seen the reports. You never came forward, either. That's because

Blackpoole was doing exactly what you wanted him to do, after you softened him up with your pharmacopeia."

"My what?"

"Drugs."

He took a backward step.

"Just like you're doing with that red-haired kid you meet with," I said.

From a distant, dark place, McDaniels said, "What do you want?"

"A confession."

"For what?"

"For turning Blackpoole into a mass murderer," I said.

"I'm telling you, I didn't have anything—"

"You were kicked out of Yale for plagiarism."

Now his left leg twitched.

"The prof who nailed you was Rexford Chamberlain," I said.

A big, slow gulp bobbed his Adam's apple. I didn't need Joey Feint to interpret that for me.

"You unleashed Blackpoole like your own private Doberman," I said. "Trained to kill. And you sent him after my father."

McDaniels's eyes went crazy wide.

My error was self-satisfaction. I had him, I knew it, but I let him move first.

He practically jumped behind his couch and bent down, and came up with a Samurai sword.

Who keeps a Samurai sword on the floor behind his couch?

"Your scum father deserved it," he said.

Then he screamed and came at me, holding the blade in two-handed classical style.

Which meant he knew how to use it.

There is nothing mysterious about fighting a guy with a sword.

Your first order of business is to keep away from the freaking blade.

Then you have to lay into the guy so hard he can't strike again.

Both of these things I did.

He came at me over-the-top. Timing is everything, and I was in the best shape of my life. I jumped to the left, turning my body as the sword came down an inch in front of me.

I drove my left fist, the the middle knuckle taking the lead, into his right temple.

The adrenaline bath my insides were sloshing around in made that blow the most powerful I'd ever delivered, in the ring or on a heavy-bag.

McDaniels went down as if he'd been shot.

The left side of his head whammed against the corner of a table with a lamp on it.

The wrath took over, burning like a thousand blowtorches. Achilles took up the Samurai sword and brought it down in one mighty whack across the body of Thurber McDaniels. It made a sickening sound, followed by the coppery smell of blood.

I KEPT ON Neil Smoltz into the night.

He ended up at a party at a house about five miles from his own. He parked his truck on the street. I parked on the opposite side of the road and waited.

As crappy music blasted from the house, I listened to the radio. A jazz station. Time goes down a lot better with Ramsey Lewis and Dave Brubeck and Joe Sample.

A couple of hours of this. Pure glamour.

Then Smoltz came out of the house and fired up a cig. He talked and smoked with some other guy, then fist bumped him and got into his truck.

He drove. I followed.

He was heading toward the highway. I did not want him to reach it.

Burning some rubber, I passed him on the right in a move I knew would make him mad. Alpha thugs do not like being passed on the right.

He laid on his horn.

I jammed on my brakes. Heard our tires squeal. Then I put it in reverse and love-tapped his grill.

That brought him out shouting a three word query that begins with "What the ...?"

In my side-view mirror I watched him hit his chest a couple of times.

Then I got out.

The street was dark, the homes set back on big lots. No one around that I could see.

Neil repeated his question.

I said, "Sorry, man. My bad. Any damage?"

"I don't know," Neil said, looking back at his truck.

When he turned back around I popped him on the left side of his face. Not enough to put him to sleep, just to get him groggy.

I put him in the back seat and duct taped his mouth, hands, and feet.

Then I went to his truck and parked it at the curb. Locked it up like a good citizen.

Balances out kidnapping, right?

ABOUT A MILE from there, Neil Smoltz started his muffled screaming.

I pulled over on a turnout. I turned to him and said, "I'm not going to hurt you."

He screamed some more. Under the mouth tape it was pitiful. He was in a semi-fetal position but with arms taped behind his back.

"You can stop screaming," I said.

He screamed again.

"You want me to let you go?"

He nodded. In the dim light his eyes looked a scared rabbit's. I'd seen that look before, the last time I went hunting with grandfather. I never went hunting again. Smoltz's look made me almost want to take him out for a milkshake.

"If I take the tape off your mouth, will you be quiet?"

Nod.

"Nobody's around here. Nobody can hear you. Got it?"

Nod.

I tore off the tape.

He screamed. In pain.

"Sorry," I said.

"You freaking kidnapped me!"

"Listen. I'm going to let you go. I'm not going to hurt you. I'm just going to use you."

"Please man, not that!"

"It's not what you think," I said. "I just need to get some information from your father."

He took in a couple of labored and frightened breaths. "What do you mean?"

At least we were now having a rational conversation, as rational as one can be after being taped up in the backseat of a car.

"How well do you know your father's work?" I said.

"I have to pee."

"Hold it in."

"For how long?"

"Depends on how ready you are to talk," I said.

"I don't know anything that can help you."

The headlights of a car on the highway hit as it drove by. Neil tried to sit up. I pushed him back down.

"Don't try that," I said.

"Who are you?" Neil said.

"We've met."

He blinked a couple of times and tried to make out my face.

"In an alley," I said. "With your friend Gavin?"

He sucked in air like somebody who'd just been punched in the stomach. "You're going to kill me!"

"Do I look like a killer?"

"Yes!"

"Fair point. But I would think that you know killers come with all sorts of looks, don't you?"

He looked genuinely confused then. I guess that he did not know about his father. That his father was trying to do everything he could to protect his son from the knowledge of what he did for a living. A real living. I decided to let it go. The kid would have to find out on his own. And when he did, I hoped he had enough money for a good psychiatrist.

"But if you really knew me," I said, "you would know that I never kill people unless I'm really angry. I hope that's a comfort to you."

He groaned and curled up even tighter.

"Another way you can keep from making me angry is to be right upfront with me. I'm very nice to people who are upfront with me."

"Gavin got a concussion."

"Then you shouldn't pull knives on people," I said.

More headlights. This time it was a car slowing down to pull into the same turnout.

I started the car and pulled out.

"I have to pee!" Smoltz said.

"Strength," I said.

.   .   .

I DO HATE to come between a man and his bladder. I pulled off the freeway onto a stretch of road without lights but a lot of trees. I stopped on the shoulder, got out, and tore the duct tape off Smoltz's wrists and ankles.

"Okay, I'm going to let you out and you're going to step over to the bushes and relieve yourself. Do not try to run away. That will make me angry. Got it?"

"Yes!"

The moon was beautiful over San Francisco across the bay. A night for lovers.

Or kidnappers.

I helped Smoltz out. Holding onto the back collar of his shirt, I led him down a slight incline to a thatch of brush. I let him go and took a couple steps back.

"Have at it," I said.

He did, with a combination of whimpers and big sighs.

When he was finished, he zipped up and turned toward me. Then with a quickness that was part natural, part fear, he turned and ran into the night screaming, "Help me!"

I WANTED TO bay at the moon. My mistake for trusting human nature. Hadn't I learned anything from Machiavelli? The whole history of philosophy should have carved all of that out of me. So why did I do it this time? Maybe it was just for the kid. He was still a kid to me, still potential, about to become one of the world's worst people. Maybe I just couldn't stand seeing another one bite that dust.

He was off and running and shouting and I had to go on afterburners to catch him. Which I did about forty yards later.

When I reached him I simply pushed him in the back and

furthered his momentum. He lost control of his legs and flew face down into the dirt and brush.

I took a knee next to him. He was crying.

"You're gonna kill me," he managed to say.

"You really think you're going to die?"

"Yes."

"Good. Feel it. Feel it all the way down to your toes. Because you know what, Neil? Someday, and probably sooner rather than later, you're going to run into another guy like me, only not as nice. That guy is the one who is going to kill you."

"What are you talking about, man?"

"How old are you, Neil?"

"Huh?"

"How old?"

"What's that matter?"

I grabbed his hair and pulled him up to a sitting position. He yelped.

"It matters because I say it does, Neil. You don't have any say here. I could take your clothes off and throw you into a bush if I wanted to."

He wiped his nose with the back of his hand.

"But I don't want to, Neil. And I won't. If you talk to me, and if I like what you say."

"You're gonna kill me, I know it."

"How old are you, Neil?"

"Twenty."

"Jeez."

"What?"

"What a waste of a life."

"What do you care, man?"

"What's your favorite car, Neil?"

"Man!"

"Come on, what is it?" Just for emphasis, I grabbed his hair again.

"Charger! Dodge Charger!"

"Good car," I said, letting go of his mop. "Now suppose somebody got a Dodge Charger, brand new, a gift, and then went out and purposely drove it into a wall. Then backed up and did it again and again until it didn't run anymore."

"What is this?" Neil said.

"Pretty stupid thing to do, right? Wasteful. That's you. But it's worse, because you hurt people while you're wrecking your own life. You're a double whammy. I don't like that. I don't like waste, and I don't like people getting hurt."

He closed his eyes and shook his head.

I tweaked his cheek.

His eyes snapped open.

"You give me your full attention," I said. "Stop wrecking your car, or you'll end up in the crusher at the junkyard. You've been warned."

At least he nodded. I'd done my duty.

"Now, Neil, before I let you go, you're going to give me a name."

"What name?"

"The name of whoever contacted you to find me and follow me that night."

Even in the dim light I could see his Adam's apple bob.

"Nobody," he said.

"Neil, look. I know what your father does. I know he has connections. I'm guessing one of them contacted you."

"No, man, really."

"Uh-huh. Suppose I take your phone and track a few of your numbers? I have a friend, he's great with computers, used to be in Israeli intelligence. Can find anything. Maybe one or two of those names would like to know you ratted them out to the cops."

"But I didn't."

"Aha."

Neil cursed.

"So," I said, "you can just give me the name now and no more will be said. Then I'll let you go."

"You'll let me go?"

"That's what I just said."

"How can I trust you?"

"Look at my face," I said. "That's a face you can trust."

"It really isn't, man."

"Hoc opus, hic labor est," I said.

"What the—"

"It's Latin, Neil. It means this is the tough part. You're going to have to talk or start taking your clothes off."

"I'm tired of this, man. I can't think."

"The name. Now."

He shook his head.

So I got his head into a reverse leg lock, which pinned him to the ground, his head behind me, his flailing torso below. I started to unbutton his shirt.

Neil's arms flopped around. "No, man, no!"

"The name!"

That's when he started to talk.

BEING A CHARITABLE man, I gave Neil Smoltz his truck keys.

But not his phone.

He did not think me a charitable man.

"Do you know the story about the woman caught in adultery?" I said.

"What the f—"

"Easy now," I said. I had him sitting on the dirt, fifty yards from the road. The silvery light made his face look ghostly. "When Jesus stepped between the woman caught in adultery, and the crowd about to stone her, he said to them, Let he who is without sin cast the first stone. And nobody could. They all went away."

"Come on, man, give me my phone."

"But here's the last part of the story," I said. "Jesus said to the woman, Go and sin no more. And that's my advice to you, Neil. You're a punk. And if you keep on being a punk, you're going to grow into a thug. I'm telling you, go and punk no more. That's my gift to you."

I stood.

"What're you doing?" he said.

"I have to go now."

"What about me?"

"You're only about a mile from the 24," I said. "Somebody will give a nice kid like you a ride."

"My phone!"

"I'll mail it to you," I said. "I promise."

WHEN I GOT to the edge of Berkeley I pulled over and called Ira.

"The city lights are lovely tonight," I said.

"Where are you?"

"I'm on a hill in Berkeley."

"What are you doing on a hill in Berkeley?"

"Well, I kidnapped a guy and threw him in my car, then let him go and drove up here for the view."

Pause.

"Ira?"

"What was that first part again?"

"Kidnapping a guy?"

"Please tell me you're just trying to get my goat," Ira said.

"I want you to keep your goat, Ira."

Pause.

"Ira?"

"I'm waiting."

I told him what happened. Every now and then Ira sighed.

After I finished, Ira said, "I want you to come back to L.A. and start working as a street sweeper."

"After I finish the job, Ira."

Pause.

"Then listen," Ira said. "That girl you're looking for, Leeza Edgar?"

"Yeah?"

"I merged a couple of records and I'm pretty sure that's not her real name."

"Do tell," I said.

"I believe she may be Lisa Ann Walsh, arrested on possession of cocaine five years ago, in San Mateo. Didn't serve time, went into a drug diversion program. I've got her last known address here."

"Give it to me."

He did, then said, "And that lawyer, Gail Goodman, I told you about."

"Agent for those shell corporations."

"You're going to find what I tell you now quite interesting."

"Quite?" I said.

"Very," he said.

He was right.

"YOUR CAMPAIGN'S DIRTY," I said.

The three of us—me, Kat, and Jay J. Parsons were in his office. It was ten in the morning, the sky was clear outside.

Inside a fog was hovering over Parsons's face.

He looked at Kat, back at me. Then laughed.

"Every campaign is dirty," he said. "Where have you been?"

To Kat I said, "You believe that?"

"Well, Mike, it is a pretty tough business."

"Fighting in a cage is a pretty tough business," I said. "But you get eliminated when you cheat."

"Come on," Parsons said. "What is all this? You work for Johnson?"

"I work for a lawyer," I said. "And what you are doing is called illegal."

"What is?" Parsons said.

"Setting up defamation," I said, "then killing people when things start to go south."

"You have any idea what he's talking about?" Parsons said to Kat.

Kat shook her head.

"I'm talking about a ham-fisted attempt to smear another campaign with a bogus story, and then killing the source."

"You're out of your mind," Parson said. "T'Kia Wilson was brought to us by Sylvia Alton. You think it was a set-up, talk to Sylvia."

"Somebody paid T'Kia Wilson," I said, "but she wasn't happy with the payment. She was demanding more and was threatening to blow the whole thing."

"How do you know that?" Kat said.

"I find people and talk to them," I said.

"Like you found me," she said.

I let that one slide.

"Look," Parsons said, "we had nothing to do with T'Kia Wilson."

"Except happily exploiting the story," I said.

"Well, what would you do, Galahad?" Parsons said. "You get a story like that, a witness like that, you've got to run with it." He pounded his index finger into the palm of his other hand. "It would be malpractice for a campaign to ignore that."

"Without fact-checking?" I said.

"Not our job," Parsons said.

I looked at Kat. "Funny, you said the same thing."

"What is all this about?" Kat said. "What can we possibly do?"

"You can issue a press release apologizing to Samuel Johnson," I said. "And his family. And his campaign. You can say that the information you now have is that T'Kia Wilson's story was false."

Parsons laughed. More like a derisive snort. "You're dreaming."

"What's stopping you?" I said.

"First of all, I don't know who you are or what you think you know. I'm not going to take your word for anything. In fact, I don't know why I'm here."

"Because you two are going to help me find out what really happened."

"Hey!" Parsons said. "I'm not doing anything with you, got that? This has nothing to do with us."

"I can always go to the reporters with what I have," I said. "But if you got ahead of this, you might actually control the damage." I looked at Kat. "That's your job, too, isn't it?"

She looked at the floor.

"There's no way," Parsons said.

"I'm actually giving you a break," I said.

"And why would you do that?"

"Maybe because I like one of the two of you," I said.

Kat looked up. I think she was fighting a smile.

"Set up a meeting with Sylvia Alton," I said. "We'll all go in and have a little chat."

Parsons said, "What do you think that's going to do?"

"We won't know until we get there," I said.

"She's not going to be very happy right now," Parsons said. "I don't even know if she'll consent to a meeting."

"Use your powers of persuasion, Jay J. That's what you're known for, right?"

. . .

WHILE PARSONS WAS making the call, Kat talked to me outside his office.

"Be careful," she said. "You don't want to mess with Sylvia Alton."

"I don't mess with anybody," I said. "I just try to have a nice, calm, rational conversation."

"Right." She shook her head. Then leaned against the wall. Tired.

"Maybe politics is not your game," I said.

Kat said, "What?" She said it like she'd been shaken from a deep sleep.

"Ever thought about that?" I said.

"It's what I do."

"It's who you are. Do you like being who you are?"

"Yeah, I do." Defiant. "And you?"

"Work in progress," I said.

Parsons came out of the office.

"Now," he said.

TEN MINUTES LATER a limo longer than it needed to be pulled in front of the campaign office. We were waiting on the street.

The limo driver, NFL-linebacker size, brought his stoic face around to us and opened the door. We got in.

Sylvia Alton was on her phone. She put up a hand, keeping us silent.

But she looked me in the eye.

Sylvia Alton was seventy-four years old, but looked like a vibrant fifty. In part it was the way she was dressed, which was perfectly, as if she had a staff dedicated only to matching her clothes, nail polish, makeup and earrings.

She wore a white suit with a blood-red blouse.

"No," she said into the phone. "That is unacceptable."

What I knew about Sylvia I'd learned with two hours of research the night before. She had come a long way since setting fire to her brassiere in front of an AP photographer at the intersection of Bancroft and Telegraph in Berkeley. She was a third-year at Boalt Hall law school back then, the wild and wacky sixties, and she was prompted to perform her act of undergarment arson because she'd been passed over for editor of the Law Review.

Because she was a woman, she claimed.

Sylvia was slightly older than most of her fellow law students. She'd been a wife and mother for five years previous to starting at Boalt. But in her second year she divorced Frank Alton and decided sex and raising children were outmoded conventions. There was also a slot to be filled in the feminist movement. Sylvia filled it.

And the "Burning at Berkeley" was the start, her first manipulation of the press.

It took a few years, to work her way to the front pages. Sylvia had to start local, and made her bones in the Bay Area by specializing in the burgeoning area of hostile work environments. She finally made it to national prominence when she won a huge victory against the San Jose Fire Department. When it was forced to hire its first woman, the station captain put up a Hugh Hefner All-Star Bunnies calendar.

Oops.

After that victory, Sylvia got on all the talk shows and a few years later made the cover of *Time* magazine.

Sylvia's life became a series of moments after that—photo ops, pithy interviews, but mainly legal victories. She started a boutique firm with offices in San Francisco and Los Angeles. Her office in S.F. had a flagpole. When she won a case, she ran a skull and crossbones flag up the pole to flap in the wind. It was her one-finger salute to everyone who hated her.

The limo was moving along Market Street when Sylvia

ended her call and said, "Five minutes."

"THERE ARE TWO shell corporations that own the building where T'Kia Wilson was stashed."

"That's an ugly word," Sylvia said.

"The agent for service of process is a lawyer named Gail Goodman," I said. "Know her?"

Sylvia folded her hands on her lap and just stared.

"She was your law clerk four years ago," I said. "I'm guessing you're one of the officers of one of the corporations, maybe even both. How'm I doing?"

"You're a very intrusive person," she said. "But everything is perfectly legal."

"Murder isn't legal," I said.

"What are you suggesting?"

"Some years ago a man was arrested for murder right here in the city. A zealous attorney managed an incredible feat. She got the only credible evidence suppressed. The suspect had requested a lawyer be present before questioning, but he was kept in custody while a detective tapped his call from a public phone."

"You really are intrusive," she said. "You have the gall to investigate *me?*"

"Your client's name was Adam Comapla."

"You don't have to tell me my client's name."

"I'm laying out a case here," I said. "You know all about that, don't you?"

"Finish," she said.

"Adam Comapla does not exist. Someone who looks just like him goes by the name of Orin 'Orrie' Smoltz."

The placid, ice-palace face of Sylvia Alton, the stuff of courtroom legend, cracked. Not into a crevice, but enough to see frozen mud underneath.

"I'll finish my closing argument," I said, "then submit the case to the jury." I made a little motion at the three of them.

Kat looked like a textbook illustration from a class in applied psychology, under the heading *The Conflicted Personality*.

I could have put my picture right up alongside hers.

"You will issue a statement," I said, "about having new evidence to suggest that T'Kia Wilson's story about her and Samuel Johnson was false. That her death has lifted the attorney-client privilege, and you are setting the record straight."

Sylvia turned to Parsons. "Is this man insane?"

"I warned you," Parsons said.

"Here's some free advice," I said, "which is more than you deserve. That statement will make you look good. Like an oxymoron, the honest lawyer. You can shift the blame however you want. I don't really care. What I care about is Samuel Johnson's good name, which you and this thing you call a campaign have tried to destroy. Make that statement and I won't say a word about anything of the information I have, to the cops, the feds, or an ambitious local reporter on KGO."

"A threat," Sylvia said.

"It's more along the lines of what the Gauls demanded of Rome in 390 BC," I said. "After they sacked Rome, they said they'd go away for a thousand pounds of gold. You're getting off easy."

"Who talks like this?" Sylvia said.

"He does," Kat said.

"Is he crazy?" Sylvia said.

"I don't think so," Kat said.

"You can speak directly to me, Ms. Alton," I said.

Inside the limo was a long, eight-month-pregnant pause. The pains were just kicking in.

"Wait," she said.

We rode in silence for a moment, then the limo pulled into a parking structure. A guy at the kiosk waved at us.

"My office," Sylvia said.

"You own this building, too?" I said.

She didn't answer. The limo drove down a level and pulled up in front of a stairwell.

"I want to talk to Jay J and Ms. Hogg alone," Sylvia said. "Wait here."

"Five minutes," I said, wanting to wink at her. But I didn't.

Sylvia nodded to Parsons, who opened the door. Sylvia got out first. Parsons followed.

Kat said to me, "Is this really happening?"

"You're about to have a moment of great clarity," I said.

"What does that even mean?"

"Go find out," I said.

Then I was alone in a limo. Big limo. I could have lived in it. All I need is a place to sleep, read. A monk's cell on wheels, this. And maybe that would be the best outcome of all. Mike Romeo, wandering vagabond, like Cain after he killed Abel.

After I killed McDaniels, I vagabonded back to Louisville. According to the cops in New Haven, McDaniels had been killed by an "intruder" and they were following up with a "person of interest."

No mention of interest in someone named Michael Chamberlain.

For the first year away I looked over my shoulder a lot as I trained with Demetrius Boland. He only asked me once why I changed my name to Romeo, and I told him I always liked Shakespeare. That was good with him. Jersey guys know when to leave another man's business alone.

But the business of killing a man does something to you, no matter how you try to tell yourself it doesn't. Demmy Boland knew I was different. He could see it in my eyes. And he told me whatever it was, it would either end my fighting career before it started—or turn me into somebody very dangerous.

I started going into the cage after that.

. . .

FIVE MINUTES BECAME ten. I was hoping that was because Kat was trying to talk some sense into Parsons and Alton.

And if she was, what did that mean to me?

Could I imagine Mike Romeo in San Francisco?

Doing what?

Living with a woman? The thought had never occurred to me before. When you're a walking toxicity bomb, an existential mess, you usually only think about the next day. You hope it comes. Sometimes you hope you don't wake up.

I got out of the limo and stretched.

The NFL-size driver was leaning on the hood, looking at his phone.

"How's it going?" I said.

He looked at me, nodded, went back to his phone.

"Nice day," I said.

He didn't look up.

"The underground garages are especially nice this time of year."

He kept his eyes on the phone.

The stairwell door opened.

It was not Sylvia.

Or Parsons.

Or Kat.

"You have got to be kidding," I said as Kwame Owens and two of his dogs came out, guns pointed at me.

They all wore shades.

"This is a bad move, K," I said.

One of the dogs shot me.

. . .

A FAMOUS ACTOR once said, "Dying is easy, comedy is hard."

This whole thing was a comedy, a bad one, starring Mike Romeo and three ridiculous castoffs from a bad 80s sketch show.

One of whom had a freaking tranquilizer gun.

Yeah, it was a dart that he hit me with, and all it takes is a few seconds before the drug hits the blood stream. You start falling into the warmth and the blackness.

Just before it all went dark I heard myself say, "Really?"

WHEN I CAME floating back to the surface I was cold. And outside. And lying on a cold slab.

My brain was a sock filled with loose change. The change jangled as I rolled onto my back.

Lights were on, like a stadium.

There was no roof.

"Welcome to my rock," somebody said. A figure stepped into my field of vision. With lights behind him, I couldn't make much out. It looked like he wore an overcoat all buttoned up and a wool hat on his head.

"How you feeling?" he said.

I thought I might vomit.

"Can you hear me?"

"Where am I?" I said. It sounded like somebody else, who was drunk.

"You're a guest on Alcatraz. We're all alone tonight."

It wasn't a hallucination, I knew that. It wasn't a movie. I knew that, too.

So it was some kind of reality. That realization, and the biting air, started to bring me around.

"I'm shot," I said.

"It was a tranquilizer," he said. "That's all."

"Tranquil ... you drugged me?"

"Sit up," the guy said. "Let me help you."

He put his hands under my shoulders and got me to a sitting position.

I was in the yard, I guessed. I'd never been to Alcatraz before.

Maybe the ghost of Al Capone could get me out of here.

The guy in the overcoat said, "I really wanted you to see this, Mr. Romeo."

"And you would be?"

"This was where it all started, you know. The Native American takeover in '69. Remember?"

"1969?"

"Yes."

"I wasn't exactly born yet," I said, rubbing my temples in a circular motion. My heart was beating fast.

"You should have studied it at one point," he said. "I understand you're an educated man."

Drugged and dragged to Alcatraz Island?

"Really?" I said.

"You know what the *San Francisco Chronicle* called me?" the guy said. "The Padre from Pasadena who seems to take his cadence from Martin Luther King."

"Weaver," I said.

"I'm going to turn this rock into a training ground for indigenous peoples," Father Dwayne Weaver said.

"Fab. How do I get out of here?"

"Genevieve has introduced a bill to reclaim this site for the true owners, the people who were here long before us. This place belongs to them, and we're going to give it back."

I started to get to my feet. It was an adventure. Empty passages and block buildings surrounded me. Maybe I was standing on the very spot the Birdman of Alcatraz was when he watched the seagulls.

Dwayne Weaver said. "Have you read Nietzsche?"

"Sure," I said. "He wears out his welcome."

"How do you mean?"

"Would you want him at your party?" I said, swaying a little, wondering if I should just deck him.

"Life is suffering, Mr. Romeo," he said.

"You're not a barrel of laughs yourself," I said.

"Our Lord suffered for mankind. We haven't been asked to go that far. We've only been asked to look out for the least of these, and that's something you seem to be opposed to."

"You don't know anything about me," I said.

"I know a good deal about you," Weaver said. "I know you have come to us under false pretenses."

"And how do you know that?"

Weaver stepped right into a beam of light blaring down on this old and worn piece of rock. It made him look like a soloist at the Met. "I have been appointed a prophet," he said. "I knew it from the time I was a little boy. Do great things, be part of a great movement. Along the way I've been opposed by wicked men. Sometimes wicked women. Do you know who Jezebel was?"

"Bette Davis," I said.

He frowned. "No, in the Bible. The wife of Ahab. She brought Baal worship into the kingdom of Israel. She stood against Almighty God. You can't do that and win."

"I'm just standing on a slab in an old prison. This isn't worth anybody's time."

He came up close to me. I could smell the junk he put in his hair. "You killed T'Kia Wilson," he said.

"Oh yeah?"

"You are going to make a confession."

"Sure I am. You can join me."

He snorted a laugh. Or maybe it was just a snort.

I said, "You're a beefy-faced fraud who rides racial dissatisfaction to the self-importance you never earned. Do you even believe in God?"

"I met with the Lord here years ago," he said. "He stood right over there."

Cue the cuckoo music.

"And soon you will meet him yourself," he said. To the shadows he said, "Come forth!"

Kwame Owens stepped into the light.

"Really?" I said. It was my new favorite word.

"It's something he wanted," Weaver said. "I have to keep up morale."

"That include bone-crunching a guy on drugs?"

"Whatever it takes," Weaver said.

"How very Jesus of you," I said. "Don't they have some security in this place?"

"Not tonight," Weaver said.

Kwame took off his shirt. He was ripped. Looked like he could still cripple a receiver.

"My wing's out of commission," I said.

"Not my problem," Kwame said.

"Oh, right," I said. "Dirtiest player in the league. Cheap shot on Delroy McQueen. Punk coward play."

Kwame the former Lion came at me fast, as if I was about to tuck one in from Tom Brady.

There was nothing wrong with my legs. But Kwame Owens had faced many a juke, and I only managed to get him slightly off his initial thrust. His right hand grazed my chin as I spun left. If I'd had my right arm available I would have followed up with a takedown move, over my leg. As it was, I could lift it up only halfway and it flapped in the breeze like a cape.

Kwame got into a fighting stance and started throwing punches. I pulled my head back a couple of times, Ali style, and he missed.

So it was going to be boxing. And me without a right.

Which left me the left.

Which had the bum digit, the little one that would not make a fist.

I told it to. I willed it to. My hand closed and a little kick of pain tweaked me. But it closed.

It was tight.

I had it back.

I ducked another punch and tagged Kwame with a left jab. It landed solid, on his button, and he stepped back and felt his nose with his hand. Blood.

He gave a guttural shriek and ran at me. I jumped out of his way and he missed completely. I shot him a left on the back of the head.

All that was going to do was slow him for a second or two. This wasn't going to be settled with my one, good fist, as happy as I was to see it back.

"Fight like a man!" Kwame said. Then started in with trash mouth. *Woodpecker woodpecker woodpecker.*

I had a favorite takedown move from the old days, called Flipping the Switch. But it involved landing on the mat on my back. That was not going to be pleasant on the floor of The Rock. But for that reason he wouldn't be expecting it. Kwame was an upright fighter. You can always tell. He'd be a Tyson man, not a cage man.

Just to test him, I gave him a kick to the side. Landed good but he was hard-muscled there. Still, it got his attention. He called me a female dog. The unoriginality of it was almost as bad as the fight itself.

"You should have stayed in school," I said. Kwame Owens had gone to Florida State, and turned pro after his junior year.

Kwame came at me with a good combination. Left, right, left. The left hit my shoulder, the bad one, and a lightning storm went off down my side.

I was not going to be able to keep going. He was a hundred percent. I was about sixty, and the pain would wear me down.

Dwayne Weaver stood there watching. This fine man of God had a smile on his face.

Kwame knew I was hurt, and like the dirty football player he was, he went for the weak point. I saw it in his eyes. He was going for the shoulder again.

I waited for the left to be thrown and as it came at me, I went down. My left leg shot between Kwame's, and my right leg curled around behind his own right. At the same time my back hit concrete I flipped the switch, forcing Kwame down by taking his leg out from under him.

The explosion in my shoulder was atomic. My brain erupted in flame, but a voice called out within the fire, reminding me the move was not over. I had to keep him down, had to pin him.

Under the rules, of course. But rules were on the other side of the water now. We were on Alcatraz, baby. We were in the yard where many an inmate met angry death with a shiv or a pipe or a dropped weight.

My normal move would have had me coming over him with my left arm, but that was out.

Then something popped.

I thought it was a bone at first.

Then I saw Dwayne Weaver drop to the cement. With blood on his head.

Both Kwame and I froze like some weird modern art depicting the tension between the races.

Then another pop, and Kwame's body jerked.

Somebody was shooting at us from the east side.

I rolled off Kwame, turned, and saw a figure up on the wall, lit for a moment, turning and disappearing. Did I see a rifle, too, or did my mind make that up?

Kwame groaned.

I saw he was bleeding from his right pec. I went to check on Dwayne Weaver. He was not going to give any more sermons.

Kwame moaned again. He was bad off.

I got his shirt and pressed it into the wound.

"Hold that," I said, taking Kwame's left hand and placing it over the shirt.

Then I ran into the shadows after the shooter.

It was a guessing game from there, where to go, what direction. I ended up outside a concrete wall, on high ground, looking toward Berkeley.

And heard the sound of a boat engine cranking up.

Down in the dark waters, barely visible, I could see it, blasting away from The Rock.

WITH HIS ARM around my shoulder I helped Kwame down the ramp to the boat he'd come over on with Weaver.

"Got to get you to a hospital," I said.

"No," he said. "My squad."

I got him into the boat. It was a fifty-footer, a pleasure craft with a single-level cockpit.

"You need to have this looked at," I said, laying him on a cushioned bench.

"No hospital." He took out his phone.

I grabbed it.

He made some kind of move, but the pain pushed him back. His cursing was fine.

"You were going to kill me tonight," I said.

"No, man," Kwame said. "Just talk."

"Some conversation."

"Who shot me?"

"I don't know," I lied.

"Why you helping?"

"I don't know that either," I said. "Maybe every man's death diminishes me."

"What?"

"It's a poem."

"You are one weird cracker," he said. "Gimme my phone."

"You talk to me straight up," I said.

"What about?"

"I want to know everything you know about T'Kia Wilson."

"I don't know nothin' about that," he said.

"Convince me," I said.

He gave me a long look. "I got nothin' to do with all that. They came to Shipp, who came to me. That's all. We're just security."

"What do you have to do with Weaver?"

"Shipp assigned us to him, too."

"And Sylvia Alton?"

"They one big happy family."

"You get paid?" I said.

"Course I got paid," Kwame said.

"Did Weaver know about T'Kia Wilson?"

"I don't know what he knew. He dead?"

"Yes," I said.

"Good," Kwame said. "Couldn't stand hearin' that yo-boy talk."

"I think it's that soft spot in your heart that gets to me," I said.

"You gonna gimme my phone?"

"One more question," I said. "Did Kat Hogg know about this?"

" 'Bout what?"

"You, me, Weaver, out here in this lovely spot?"

"Not much she don't know about," Kwame said.

"I mean, did she approve of it?"

"I didn't ask her. Didn't see her."

"Who knows you and Weaver brought me here tonight?"

"Nobody," Kwame said.

"Alton?"

"She left it to us."

"They're going to find Weaver's body, and they're going to find your blood. And then they're going to find you."

He thought about that. Then shrugged. "Somebody shot me. I don't know who."

"What were you doing on Alcatraz?"

"Weaver and me, lookin' it over."

"Why?"

"Place for my crew. Training."

"Might work."

"What about you?" he said. "You gonna talk?"

"No reason to, if I never see you again. I'm leaving town. You and me, we got nothing more to do with each other. We good?"

"Okay," Kwame said. "We good. But ..."

"But what?"

"I could take you, man."

I said, "Maybe someday, when I'm not on drugs and you're all patched up, we can have a nice dinner and then go find a park and settle the matter."

A slight smile cracked through Kwame's mouth. "Yeah, you are one insane mother—"

"Leave it at insane," I said.

I cast off the boat, fired it up, aimed for the city.

I LEFT KWAME in the boat and gave him his phone. I even wished him luck.

He gave me a nod, which I counted as a victory for harmony among all peoples of the Earth.

In the dimness of the night, with a wet fog hanging, I walked half an hour to Kat's apartment. My rental car was parked on the street.

It had a ticket on it. I put the ticket in the glove compartment then drove over to Oakland. I checked myself into a Motel 6 and slept in a nice orange room.

In the morning I treated myself to a jalapeño breakfast burrito at Jack-in-the-Box.

Then I treated myself further at Walmart and bought a pack of disposable Bic shavers for sensitive skin. I was feeling sensitive. Got the stuff to dress my wound, too. It was going to be tricky alone. Having Kat do it would be so much easier.

But that was not going to happen.

Back at the motel I showered and shaved and covered my ugly wound. I wanted to be presentable because I was calling on a real lady.

SABLE WILSON WAS home. She welcomed me in like a long-lost son. Her house was filled with flowers, grief offerings. Sable was dressed like always, as if going to or coming from church.

"I suppose you've heard," she said.

"About T'Kia," I said.

She nodded.

"Let's sit down," I said. I took a chair and Sable sat on the sofa. Between us was an arrangement of orange and yellow calendulas. The comfort flower.

"Sable," I said, "I came to say good-bye. And I wanted you to know something. I believe there will be justice for T'Kia."

She pondered that a moment. "She's gone. My only prayer is that her soul rest with the Lord."

"If something is about to break, I'd like to call you," I said.

"You know something?"

"Nothing certain," I said. "But if I do, I'll let you know."

"Thank you." She reached out and took my left hand, squeezed it. "Where will you go now?"

"Back to Los Angeles."

"My sister lives there," she said. "It's too fast for me."

"Do you ever visit?"

"Haven't in a long time. I'm about due. Detts, that's her name, Detts, short for Bernadette, she lives there with my great niece, Philodendron."

"Your great niece is named Philodendron?"

"That's right. Course we all call her Philly."

Now it was my turn to put a cup down. With a loud *clack*. "Philly?"

"Sounds like the city, doesn't it?" Sable said.

"Does she have a boyfriend?"

"I think so. She's a very pretty girl. Why?"

"Do you know anything about the boyfriend?"

"It's all very secret," she said, looking at her hands and rubbing them together. "That's what Detts says, anyway. I think because ..."

"Yes?"

"He's white, you see. That does not bother me one bit, but Detts, she's kind of from the old school, you see."

I stood.

"Is something wrong, Mike?"

"I have one more stop to make before I head back. Sable, I wish we could have met under happier circumstances."

She came to me and this time took my right hand in both of hers. "You remember now, get offa that fence. Come see me again if you're ever up this way."

"You can bank on it," I said.

Before I drove out of Oakland I stopped at a mailbox and dropped in a small package. It had a cell phone in it. The package was addressed to Neil Smoltz.

I'd promised him. Maybe he'd take that a sign not to keep on being a punk.

Every now and then I try to believe in unicorns.

SAN MATEO IS the sister no one notices. She sits and knits between her glamorous sibling to the north and her hard-working sister, San Jose, to the south.

And in this town there are a bevy of squat, post-war homes that were built for working men and their small families.

The one I stopped in front of was on Evergreen. It was painted a faded shade of brown with a flaking white trim. The front yard had a tired, sagging used-to-be-white picket fence surrounding patches of dandelions and dirt. A cracked brick pathway led to a crooked front door with a handle ready to fall off.

This door I knocked on.

"Is that you Francine?" a woman's voice inside said.

"Yes," I said.

The door opened.

The woman was small with thin, steel-gray hair that must have once made an uneasy alliance with a curling iron. Her face was all frown and wrinkles. She was wearing a brown-and-white poncho with a Southwestern design to it and what looked like a red wine stain over the right breast.

The smell of cigarettes and salmon was strong from inside the house.

"I'm looking for Lisa Walsh," I said.

"Nobody here by that name." She tried to close the door. I kept it open with my left.

The woman called me a very bad name.

"You must be her mother," I said.

"If you don't go right now, I'm calling the police," she said.

"You don't want the police here."

"I do! Now let go!"

I pushed the door open and went in.

"Stop!" she said.

"I'm not here to hurt anybody," I said. "Will you just listen to me? It's important. Leeza's in trouble."

"I told you, nobody here by that name!"

I gave the place a quick scour. It had a scuffed, hardwood floor. Over a fake fireplace was an ocean painting that must have come with the house and cost a whole ten dollars in 1950, frame and all. Wood paneling covered all the walls, and behind a gray-and-black speckled sofa, it was warped. On the coffee table in front of the sofa was a ripped-open bag of microwave popcorn, now empty, its burnt orange insides a testament to bad eating and even worse housekeeping.

Next to the dead bag of popcorn was a large glass ashtray, stuffed with butts. Some of the butts had filters. Some of them didn't.

"She lives with you, doesn't she?" I said.

"I am telling you, get out!"

"They're going to find her."

The woman opened her mouth, but the voice came from behind her.

"Don't move," Leeza Edgar said, stepping into the room holding a handgun pointed at me with shaky hands.

"THAT WOULD BE a very ungrateful thing to do," I said.

"How did you find me?" Leeza said.

"I took a bullet for you."

"I didn't ask you to."

"Well excuse me. Put that thing down."

The gun vibrated in her hands, both of which were on the gun.

"What are you doing here?" she said.

"I thought I'd do you a favor," I said. "Excuse me again."

"You can't do anything for me."

The woman of the house said, "Maybe we better listen to him."

"That's a great idea," I said.

Leeza hesitated and I was close to certain her trembling index finger was going to jerk the trigger.

Then she lowered the gun. It was a revolver.

"Does your mother know?" I said.

This brought an uncomfortable look between Leeza and the woman.

"Know what?" Leeza said.

"You want to talk with me alone," I said, "or in her presence?"

The woman said, "What's he talking about?"

Leeza shook her head, a defeated shake, went over to a wingback chair with a hole in one wing, sat down and put the gun on her lap. She rubbed her eyes with her palms.

"Lisa, what is this all about?" said the woman.

"Why don't you tell her?" Leeza said.

The woman looked at me. "I need a cigarette," she said.

"Me, too," Leeza said.

"Open a window," I said.

Neither one made a move to the window. Leeza took a pack of Camels out of her jeans and her mother took a pack of Marlboro Lights out of whatever she was wearing under the poncho. Leeza lit her cig with a Bic. Her mother took the Bic from her and lit her own. I looked around for an oxygen mask but didn't see one.

"Now tell it," the mother said.

"Your daughter was out on Alcatraz last night," I said.

Mom laid a dagger look on Leeza. "You didn't."

Leeza nodded a slow yes.

Mom took a drag on her cigarette that must have gone

down to her feet. She went to the speckled sofa and sat.

"Now I'm the one who's in the dark," I said.

"Maybe you should have a cigarette," Leeza said. At least she had a dark sense of humor.

"I'm ingesting two packs right now," I said. "Your mother knows?"

"I killed him," Leeza said.

"I figured," Mom said.

"Why?" I said.

"Does he know?" Mom said.

"No," I said. "I don't. Somebody just fill me in."

"I know every bit of that stupid rock," Leeza said. "Used to play there as a kid. I can get on and off whenever I want. And you want to know why?"

"That's why I'm standing here."

"Because my father took me there. It was the first place he had me. Right there in one of the old cells."

The women paused for long drags. They both had expressions like they were watching a sad movie for the fourth time and knew the ending wouldn't change.

My razor-sharp mind started rearranging pieces. I took a shot.

"Dwayne Weaver was your father?" I said.

"Bingo," Leeza said. "Give the man a cigar."

The irony of her remark was lost on her.

Her mother sank deeper into the sofa. Shoulders hunched forward, cigarette resting in the corner of her expressionless mouth.

I just waited for the next bombshell.

"I was one of a bunch of his," Mom said. "Volunteer at the soup kitchen. That's where he liked to pluck 'em. I told him I wasn't gonna have an abortion, and he was gonna do the right thing. He paid me to keep it secret. I said he had to treat her like a daughter. He did until she was ..."

"Twelve," Leeza said. "That's when it started."

"I took her away," Mom said.

"Why didn't you go to the police?" I said.

Mom snorted a laugh. "You can't fight those people. Not people like us."

"I took care of it," Leeza said.

"Where's the rifle?" I said.

"The bay."

"How'd you know he'd be out there?" I said.

"I watched his boat."

"And you have a boat?"

"A friend."

"You almost shot me, too," I said.

"I have good aim," Leeza said. "I wanted that Kwame dead, too. He made it, didn't he?"

"Yeah he did," I said. "And if he ever finds out ..."

"You gonna tell him?"

I shook my head. "But somebody might connect some dots and try to look you up. There's still a law against murder."

"It was justified," Leeza said.

"It was first-degree, special circumstances," I said.

Leeza took up the revolver again. "I'm not going to prison."

"I'm not a cop," I said.

"What are we supposed to do?" Mom said. She looked at me as if I knew.

And then I heard myself say, in a voice that seemed coming from the outside, "When you kill somebody it stays with you. Even if you get away with it. It never goes away. You carry it around inside and it can eat you up. Maybe the only thing you can do is find some way to help somebody else. Get close to one or two people, stay close to them, give part of your life to them. That might be the only way to make it."

That's what I left them with.

. . .

I WAS TEN minutes past San Jose when I called Kat.

"Oh my God, Mike, where are you?"

"I'm in a rented car heading home."

"What happened to you? Things are blowing up here."

"You know what happened to me."

"No, no. I don't. They told me nothing."

"It will all become clear to you soon, I'm sure."

"Tell me about it," she said. "Come up here and tell me. I want to see you."

"We'll always have Paris," I said.

"What are you talking about?"

"Did you ever see *Casablanca?*"

"Mike, I want to see you. When can you be here?"

"I don't have any plans to come back to San Francisco in the near future."

"You're not going to see me?"

"You need to get out of politics," I said. "Read *Moral Man and Immoral Society* by Reinhold Niebuhr."

"Will you stop talking the way you talk?"

"A group always overwhelms the individual. As long as you're in with those people, your morality's going to be messed up. Maybe you didn't know what was happening to me, but you should have. And you're part of what made it happen."

"Can't we talk about this? I still have some of your things at my place."

"Donate them."

"Mike, please. I don't want us to stop. I'll do whatever it takes."

"No, you won't."

"Where can I reach you? Maybe in a few days we can—"

"Hopefully I'll be swimming in the Pacific Ocean. If you take a boat down the coast, you might see me. Good luck, Kat."

"Mike—"

That was the last word I ever heard from Katarina Hogg.

PASSING THROUGH PASO Robles, I called Ira.

"Have they discovered Dwayne Weaver's body yet?" I said.

"Do you want to run that by me again?" Ira said.

"Father Dwayne Weaver, the padre from Pasadena, was murdered last night."

"Murdered?"

"I was there."

Pause.

"Dear God," Ira said. "Don't tell me."

"Okay," I said, "I won't. Because there's no need. I didn't do it."

"But you were there?"

"I should be back in L.A. in about four hours. I want you to arrange a meeting. With the heads of the five families."

"The who?"

"You, Steadman, Ricky, and me."

"That's only four."

"Make sure Ricky is there," I said. "I don't care how you do it, but make it happen."

"Do you want to brief me on this?"

"Let it be a surprise," I said.

"You are full of surprises," Ira said.

"You have no idea," I said.

It was a beautiful day to drive. The sky was blue and clear, unlike the last canopy I was under in San Francisco. The hills to the west were green, fresh from recent rains. By the time I passed Buellton the sun was on the second half of its arc.

And then I came to the ocean. It was calm today, no wind. A giant rock sat close to shore, covered with the white excrement of countless seagulls. It reminded me that natural beauty smacks up right alongside natural dirt. And the secret of life is keeping as much seagull stuff off you as possible.

WE MET IN Teodor Steadman's corner office on the third floor of the building on Wilshire. Me, Ira, Steadman and Ricky. Ricky was dressed in his Friday-casual hipster outfit, an unbuttoned oversized flannel shirt with a puce tee underneath, skinny jeans, and yellow high-top Converse.

I sat in a chair next to Ira. Steadman sat behind his desk. Ricky stood with his arms folded, unsmiling.

Steadman smiled and reached over his desk to shake my hand.

"You are a stud," he said.

"I think maybe we should use another word," I said.

"What would that be?"

"How about patsy?" I said.

Steadman shook his head.

I said, "Patsy, noun, somebody set up by somebody else, to be cheated or take a fall."

Steadman looked confused. "Why would you say that?"

"Because that's what happened to me," I said.

Blank stare. Then Steadman said, "Are you saying you think I did something to set you up?"

"Not you," I said.

I looked at Ricky.

He unfolded his arms.

"What's this all about?" Steadman said.

"I got no idea," Ricky said.

"Why don't you have a seat, Ricky?" I said.

"Why don't you blow it out your—"

I shot to my feet, faced him.

"All right," I said, "we'll do this standing up."

"This is nuts," Ricky said, taking a step back.

"You ever heard of SWIFT?" I said.

"Who?" Ricky said.

"Society for Worldwide Interbank Financial Telecommunication," I said.

Ricky shook his head.

"Tell him, Ira," I said.

"It's an international banking network," Ira said. "Hard to crack. Not impossible."

"So?" Ricky said.

"Sylvia Alton is a principal in two shell corporations," Ira said. "Both of them have bank accounts in Aruba. I mentioned this little bit of information to Mike."

I smiled.

Ricky shifted from side to side.

"What is going on?" Teodor Steadman said.

"When I first met with Ricky," I said, "his girlfriend was here. Philly. Full name, Philodendron. They were having a lover's quarrel because Ricky was being an ass. She made an offhand remark about going to Aruba alone. Half an hour ago I talked to Philly on the phone."

"You did what?" Ricky said.

"She didn't call you about it?" I said.

"No," he said.

"Maybe you two need some counseling."

"Why don't you shove it up your—"

"She said you're leaving in a couple of weeks," I said. "For Aruba."

"Oops," Ira said.

"So what?" Ricky said.

"It's circumstantial evidence," Ira said. "The direct evidence is your IP address, linked to a contact with the bank in Aruba that services the shell corporations."

There is a look that a fourteen-year-old gets when his parents show him the pipe and nickel bag they found in his underwear drawer. A desperate eye slide, accompanied by short breaths.

Ricky had that look now.

To Steadman I said, "Let's have a look at Ricky's phone and tablet. I'd be willing to bet Ricky a new pair of shoes that we'll find a connection to a man named Orrie Smoltz. He is a key player in our little scenario. A killer, in fact."

"I don't have to take this," Ricky said, and huffed. He started for the door. Ira reached out and grabbed the back of Ricky's flannel shirt, yanked, and Ricky was on his keister on the floor. Then Ira wheeled himself in front of the door and crossed his arms.

Ricky got up, red-faced and cursing.

Teodor Steadman stood. "I want to know what this is about!"

I said, "Ricky found out about a desperate girl named T'Kia Wilson, through his girlfriend, who happens to be her cousin. He used Orrie Smoltz to get to Sylvia Alton to suggest a little dirty trick to play on the Johnson campaign. Pay this girl to give a fake story about Johnson."

Steadman looked at his son as if waiting for an answer.

Ricky didn't say anything.

Steadman said, "Is this true?"

"Of course not," Ricky said.

I said, "My guess is that T'Kia Wilson started asking for more money and threatened to blow the whole scheme. I think Ricky thought it would be best to shut her up for good. And you know what else?"

Silence, though Ricky was definitely giving off the scent of fear.

"I don't think Philly knows any of this," I said. "When she finds out, it's going to put a real damper on the relationship."

"Why would you do this?" Steadman said to Ricky.

"I didn't do anything!" he said.

"I can hazard a guess," I said.

The two Steadmans looked at me.

"May I?" I said.

"May you what" Steadman said.

"Hazard a guess."

"Yeah, yeah," Steadman said.

"I'm not a licensed family therapist," I said, "but I think there's been more than a little tension in your nest."

"Nest?" Steadman said. "What are you talking about?"

"May I speak freely?"

"Yes! Please!"

"When we first met," I said to Steadman, "you made some comments about your ex-wife."

He looked confused.

"Hitler's daughter?" I said.

"Oh that," Steadman said. "Just blowing off steam."

"Nasty divorce?"

"So?"

"Because you came out as gay?"

It was like the room filled with ice. Steadman's face got hot enough to melt it. But he didn't say anything.

"You dropped some subtle lines on me," I said. "Asking me out for a drink with a wink in your voice. I told you I drank alone. Remember?"

"So what of it? I don't see that has anything to do with all this."

"Maybe Ricky has some unspoken animosity about what happened between you and his mother, and the reasons for it. I'm just spit-balling here. But as Tolstoy said, 'each unhappy family is unhappy in its own way.' A son taking down a father is one of those ways."

"Why are we even listening to this?" Ricky said.

I said, "Because somebody has to pay for the murder of Sable Wilson's granddaughter."

"Who is Sable Wilson?" Steadman said.

"A friend," I said.

"He's crazy," Ricky said.

Teodor Steadman froze for a moment, his face tortured. Then he looked at Ricky. "Let me see your phone."

"What?" Ricky said.

"We're going to examine it."

"No way!"

"Yes, Ricky! Now."

A slow but noticeable trembling came over Ricky Steadman. He had six pairs of eyes on him and he felt every one.

He looked toward the door, where Ira was stationed. He looked at me, then his father.

I still don't know if Ricky was trying to kill himself or just get out of there, even from three stories up. All I know is what I saw—Ricky took two steps and threw himself at the office window.

THERE ARE STORIES that end in tragedy. The hero is killed, or murdered, or commits suicide. Various methods have been employed by the playwrights through the centuries. Shakespeare preferred swords and daggers. Chekov liked guns.

Then there is comedy.

In Teodor Steadman's office, we got a scene which was a little of both, and I couldn't help smiling.

Ricky Steadman did not break the tempered glass of his father's office window.

Instead, he bounced off it, fell on the floor and writhed in pain, holding his shoulder.

To Teodor Steadman I said, "I think you two have some things to talk over."

. . .

IRA TOOK ME to lunch at Philippe's, the French-dip sandwich place across from Union Station.

"We make a pretty good team," Ira said as we sat and dipped and ate.

"Do we?"

"My good looks and experience, along with your brawn," Ira said.

"Unbeatable," I said.

"How bad do you have it?" Ira said. "I mean about the woman in San Francisco."

"I cut it off before it got bad," I said. "I'm pretty good at that."

"Maybe you need to let things hurt a little bit more."

"The point being?"

"That's what makes life sweet. What about that woman at the bookstore? What was her name?"

"I don't recall," I said.

"Michael, I am not someone who lies," Ira said. "You owe me the truth."

"Her name is Sophie," I said.

"Maybe you should drop by and say hello."

"Maybe you should dip your sandwich and eat," I said.

That's exactly what Ira did.

As he chomped, some words came to me and I couldn't get them out of my head.

"What is it?" Ira said.

"A complete accord on all subjects human and divine," I said, "joined with mutual goodwill and affection."

Ira blinked.

"Cicero on friendship," I said. "I owe you that, too. So I want to tell you about it. Everything."

"About what?"

"What happened in New Haven. About what I did there, after my parents died. I hope you're ready for it."

"With you, Michael, I believe I am now ready for anything."

"Maybe you speak too soon."

"Try me."

So I told him.

Everything.

When I finished I felt like I'd been turned inside out, scraped and hosed, then put back again.

Ira, who had seen and heard much worse in his years with Mossad, looked at me with eyes full of perfect understanding. There was mercy in them, too. Not the begrudging kind, but the kind that lights a candle in the darkest cave, and beckons you toward the way out.

TWO DAYS LATER Samuel Johnson and his wife, Iris, came by Ira's house.

"I just wanted to thank you," he said.

"No need," I said.

"But there is. He who steals my purse steals trash—"

I said, "But he that filches my good name robs me of that which not enriches him, and makes me poor indeed."

"*Othello*," Samuel Johnson said.

"Iago," I said. "He has all the good lines."

Iris Johnson gave me a hug and thanked me, too.

"You heard they arrested Ricky," Johnson said.

"Yes."

"Teodor told me he wants to get out of politics. Wants to go get his Masters in Thanatology."

"Death and dying," Ira said.

"That'll cheer him up," I said.

Johnson said, "Leaving me to go forward on my own. The press is not going to be great."

Ira said, "The good news is most people don't think the press is that great, either."

"Good luck," I said.

"I don't expect I'll win," Johnson said. "After all, this is California. But sometimes lost causes are the only causes worth fighting for."

"*Mr. Smith Goes to Washington*," I said.

"That's right," Johnson said, beaming. "One of my favorite movies."

"May life imitate art," I said.

"Would you consider working with me, on the campaign?" Johnson said.

"I don't mix well with politics," I said. "I find compromise a challenge."

"Truer words were never spoken," Ira said.

THE FOLLOWING TUESDAY I knocked on a door.

Henry's mother answered. She was surprised to see me. She almost closed the door, but said, "What do you want?"

"May I ask how Henry is doing?" I said.

She opened her mouth, stopped, looked down. I thought she might cry.

"I don't want to intrude," I said.

Shook her head again, slowly.

"Is he still being bullied?" I asked.

She nodded.

"Has the school done anything?"

"No."

"Henry has the right to defend himself. I can teach him how to do that. Not to be the aggressor. Only to stop the aggression. I would be happy to do that."

"But who are you? I don't know anything about you."

"I'm your neighbor," I said. "And you know what? If you let

me help Henry, you'll be helping somebody else."

"Who?

"Me."

She let me in.

THE NEXT MORNING I woke up while it was still dark and pulled on my running stuff and headed up toward the hills. Feet pounding pavement, the city just waking up. A couple of cars passed me, headlights streaming. And I thought about what I would do if I could run and not get tired. If I could keep running, where would I go?

Maybe a stretch of road through a desert, long and straight, going and going as far as that would take me—hello Texas, hello Kentucky, hello Atlantic Ocean—and then what? Catch a boat?

Or I could run back to the city, to mix it up again in the ragged way of life, no certainty to it, pain and betrayal in it, but also people, like Ira, who would never betray me. And Henry and his mother who, in some small way, needed me.

And from a distant mental canyon in my brain, the name Sophie reverberated like a soft echo.

I ran and ran.

Upward I ran, finally getting to a thin strip of road along an undeveloped ridge. I stopped where the scrub and weeds were heavy, sweet-scented in the thin layer of mist. The first light of morning, orange-yellow, painted the sky, and I saw the shadowy outline of the buildings downtown.

I stood there for a few minutes and breathed in and out and watched, and as the sky got brighter, I found myself turning around, running again, down, down, down, back toward Ira's house.

Back to the world.

To stay.

AUTHOR'S NOTE

Thank you for reading *Romeo's Way*. The other books in the series are: *Romeo's Rules, Romeo's Hammer, Romeo's Fight*.

There's more to come. And if you'd like to be on my email list and be among the first to know when the next one's coming, please go to JamesScottBell.com and navigate to the FREE book page. I won't share your email address with anyone, nor will I stuff your mailbox with spam. It's just a short, to-the-point email from time to time.

Meanwhile, I have another suspense series featuring lawyer Ty Buchanan. The books are:

Try Dying (Ty Buchanan Legal Thriller #1)

Try Darkness (Ty Buchanan Legal Thriller #2)

Try Fear (Ty Buchanan Legal Thriller #3)

For all my books, for both readers and writers, see www.jamesscottbell.com.

Thanks!

Romeo's Way is a work of fiction. Though real locations are used or mentioned, events that take place are made up for the purpose of the story. All of the characters are fictional, and any resemblance to any person, living or dead, is purely coincidental.

Made in the USA
Middletown, DE
11 March 2021

34740437R00146